· DARK MOUNTAIN ·

BOOK 20

CRAIG HALLORAN

Dragon Wars: Dark Mountain - Book 20

By Craig Halloran

Copyright © 2021 by Craig Halloran

Dragon Wars is a registered trademark

TWO-TEN BOOK PRESS

PO Box 4215, Charleston, WV 25364

ISBN Paperback: 979-8485440-69-2

ISBN Hardback: 978-1956574-06-7

WWW.DRAGONWARSBOOKS.COM

All rights reserved. No part of this publication may be reproduced, stored in a retrieval system, or transmitted in any form or by any means—electronic, mechanical, recorded, photocopied, or otherwise—without the prior permission of the copyright owner, except by a reviewer who may quote brief passages in a review.

Publisher's Note

This book is a work of fiction. Names, characters, places, and incidents either are the product of the author's imagination or are used fictitiously, and any resemblance to actual persons, living or dead, events, or locales is entirely coincidental.

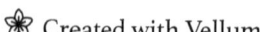

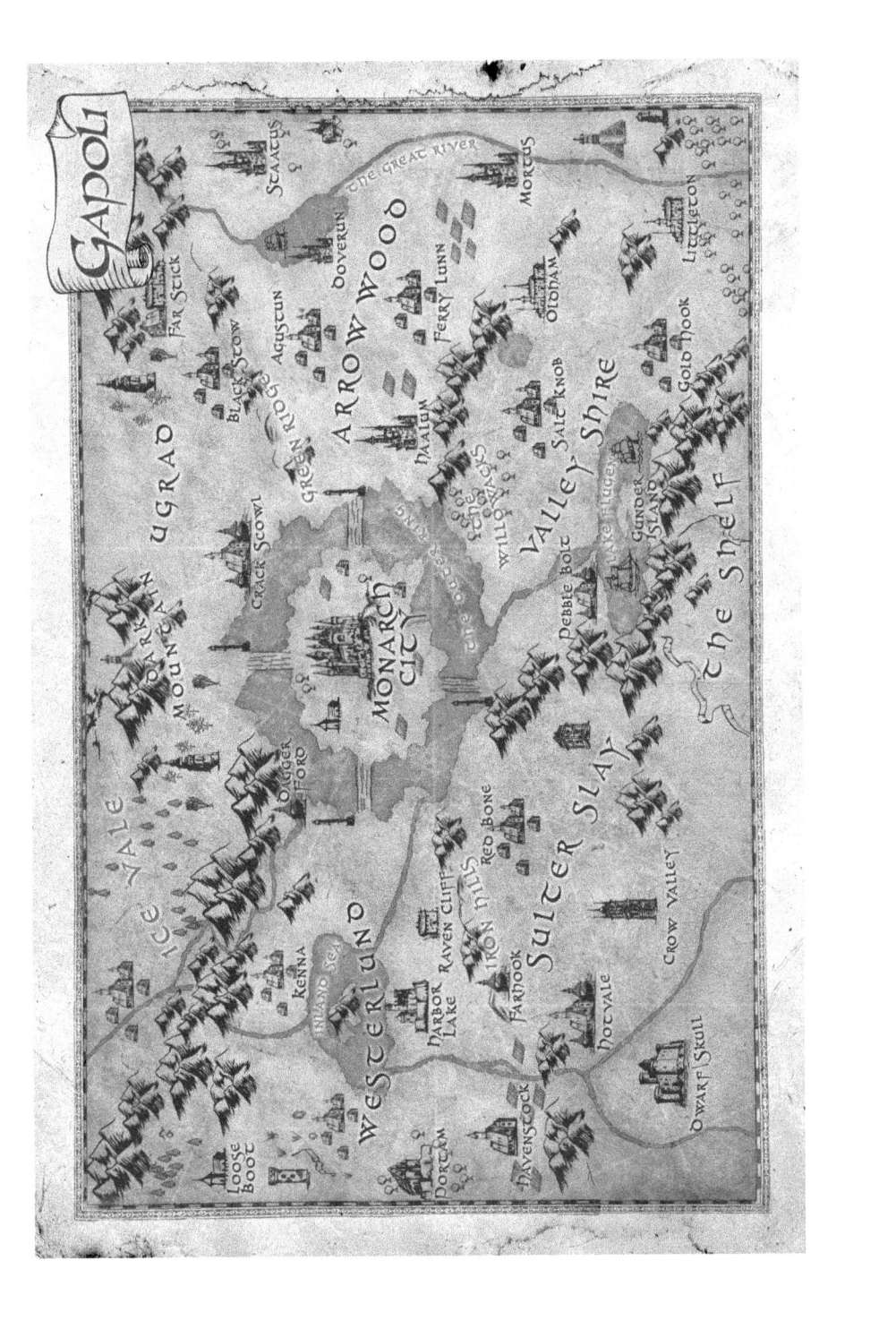

1

SULTER SLAY

The wind whistled in Grey Cloak's ears. Atop his dragon, Streak, his long black hair streamed behind his head. His smile was wide enough to catch a melon. No more than a minute ago, the situation had been dire, their chances for survival slim.

Commander Azzark, the leader of the Riskers controlling Dwarf Skull, had had the heroes pinned against the rocks. It would have been a fight to the last man. Ten Riskers and ten dragons had faced Grey Cloak and his allies—Dyphestive, Zanna Paydark, Shannon, Crane, Lythlenion, and Rhonna with her four dwarfsmen.

Grey Cloak's smile faltered as he relived the near-fatal incident. *I can't believe we made it!*

They'd been out of resources. His and Zanna Paydark's wizard fire was all but spent, the powers of the Figurine of

Heroes extinguished. The deadliest killers in the world closing in.

Streak barrel-rolled and attacked a middling dragon with his breath. It roared as Streak's flame set its tail on fire. At the same time, the enemy dragon's rider twisted around the saddle and fired an enchanted arrow, a dead-on shot for Grey Cloak's chest.

Without thinking, Grey Cloak snatched the missile from the air and gave it a curious look.

"Good catch!" Streak said as he bore down on the dragon.

Grey Cloak flicked the arrow aside like a toothpick and watched the wide-eyed Risker nock another arrow.

I really can't believe we made it! Grey Cloak exhaled as he remembered the close call.

It had all happened like a dream. Another host of dragons flew like a colony of bats, emerging from caves toward the company's spot in the hills. He'd thought for certain more of Black Frost's forces had come. He couldn't have been happier to be so wrong.

Led by Anya the Sky Rider and her grand dragon, Cinder, the remaining forces of Talon arrived like sunbeams from the heavens. The children of Cinder, with Zora, Gorva, and Reginald the Razor on their backs, made a thunderous arrival that shook the sky. The dragons were geared up for war, their riders fully clad in the armor of the Sky Riders. It was a sight of glory.

Streak chomped down on the dragon's flaming tail and gave it a fierce yank. The dragon twisted around and spat fire.

Zooks, this is getting serious.

Grey Cloak covered himself in the Cloak of Legends, stood in the stirrups, and climbed on top of the saddle. He raced up Streak's neck, planted a foot on his skull, then leaped toward the enemy rider.

The Risker let his bowstring loose.

Grey Cloak batted the shaft aside with a swipe from the Rod of Weapons. He landed on the enemy dragon's back then thrust the butt of his weapon into the orcen Riskers' chin.

"Gah!" the orc roared. Scowling, the orc snatched the rod in an iron grip and tugged Grey Cloak right into him. He busted Grey Cloak in the side of the jaw with his helmet.

Grey Cloak's knees wobbled. He heard the enemy's steel scrape out of his sheath.

Wake up, Grey! He hopped back as a shimmering blade of a dagger ripped across his belly. Maintaining his grip on the rod, he and the brute in the saddle started a tug of war.

"Yer an elf!" the snarling Risker said. "I love killing elves! Their bones break easy!"

With renewed energy that came upon his friends' arrival, Grey Cloak summoned his wizard fire. "Well, prepare to get a charge out of trying to kill this one." He sent a wave of energy through the rod that shot like fire up the Riskers' arms.

The orc's eyes brightened like blue flames. His helmet popped from his head, and his short strands of hair started to smoke. "Aaaargh!" He held on to the rod a moment longer before jerking away, his hands smoking.

Grey Cloak spun the rod around his body in a full swing like a club. Once the head blossomed into a ball of spiked energy, he made quick contact with the orc's skull.

The side of the Riskers' face caved in. He fell from the saddle like he'd been hit by an anvil.

Grey Cloak leaned over the struggling dragon's wing. "I hope he doesn't land on one of us." He raised his voice. "Streak! Take care of this one! I'm going to the surface."

Streak nodded. "You got it, boss! I'll catch up with you."

Grey Cloak jumped with an aerial somersault and plummeted below. The Cloak of Legends billowed out, and his descent quickly slowed. "Goy, we are really high up. At least a thousand feet."

Below his feet, he spotted several skirmishes taking place over the burnt and broken land of Sulter Slay. Glowing arrows and javelins streaked through the sky. Dragon flame erupted. Mighty roars exploded. Scale and bone crashed against metal. Joints in armor and bones popped and cracked. Pyres of flame and smoke rose from the ground.

It sounds bad. Maybe I should remain up here. Grey Cloak chuckled to himself.

He spied the forces on the ground. Dyphestive and the grand dragon Rock were on the move, crashing down the hills and bearing down on Commander Azzark's ground forces. Dyphestive and Rock were brutes cut from the same cloth, both musclebound in their own way.

Grey Cloak made a quick count. All of Cinder's children had come to their rescue, aside from the middling dragon triplets. The numbers were on their side for a change.

After all we've been through, do we really have the advantage?

In all directions, there was no sign of enemy reinforcements.

But Grey Cloak knew better. *There's always something. Somewhere. Where could it be?*

A dragon with a broken neck dropped from above and zoomed by Grey Cloak in a whoosh.

He glanced up angrily. "Watch what you're doing, Streak!"

Streak glided right underneath him. "Sorry, boss."

Grey Cloak made a soft landing in the saddle. "Keep an eye out for any surprises."

"Really? I love surprises."

"Not that kind," he replied. "The killer kind."

Streak nodded. "Oh."

2

Jaws clenching, Anya set her eyes on the biggest target she saw first. A Risker rode a grand splashed with pale-blue scales. Smoke streamed out of the beast's nostrils as it locked eyes with them.

"I take it we are attacking the big one?" Cinder casually asked.

"Need you ask?" Anya said as she charged up the javelin in the palm of her hand with wizard fire.

"Merely being polite." Cinder spread his wings and curved toward the enemy. "With a female fighter like you, this should be interesting."

The Risker nocked an arrow.

"What's that supposed to mean?" Anya asked.

"I'm used to you fighting larger opponents. This one is slight of build."

Anya paid more attention to the dragon than the rider with white hair flowing out of the bottom of her helmet. Anya tilted her head. "She looks old."

"The older, the wiser. Be careful." Cinder started into a slow circle a few dozen feet above the enemy.

The Risker's dragon mirrored their movements, all parties locking their eyes on one another. An elven woman rode in the saddle. Her legs were long and bare from midthigh up. Her snug armor perfectly fit her athletic body. Beneath the ridge of her open-faced helm were a pair of beautiful green eyes that reflected the sunlight like fire.

"Merza," Anya uttered. Since she was a child, she'd heard the stories about great Riskers and Sky Riders alike. Merza, though old, was one of them. There was no mistaking the woman, as her captivating features had been well described as unforgettable by all.

"Did you say something?" Cinder asked.

"Yes, that's Merza. I've heard of her before." She paused when Merza nodded at her. A chill shot down on Anya's neck. "They say she's crafty. Be careful. And her dragon—"

"Yes, I know him now. That is Fog. Crossed with him ages ago." Cinder snorted. "Finally, I can get another shot." His lips pulled back, revealing his teeth. "He won't slip by me again."

Merza managed a razor-thin smile, winked, then fired her arrow. The missile sailed below Cinder's belly, missing the dragon by the length of a man.

"She must be old. She missed you by a league." Anya raised

the javelin and cocked back her arm. "It's best we end this quick."

Thuk!

Anya arched back. "Auugh!" A piercing, hot pain bit in-between her shoulder blades. The javelin fell free of her fingers. Twisting her head over her shoulder, she saw Merza's arrow sticking in her back. "Impossible! How did she do that?"

Cinder craned his head back and with a worried look said, "Are you wounded?"

"My pride is." She glared at Merza, who politely smiled as she loaded another arrow. "She fires arrows that can bend through the air!"

That time, Merza fired high above Anya's head. The arrow whistled into the sky and vanished.

She looked about. "Where'd it go?"

Thuk! The arrow came out of nowhere and blasted into the meat of Anya's shoulder.

"Horseshoes! Not again! Cinder, get us out of here!"

Cinder flapped his outstretched wings and rose toward the clouds. Below, Merza and Fog followed at a slow pace.

Gritting her teeth, Anya snapped the shaft of the arrow buried in her shoulder. She strained to reach the one in her back and did the same. "Guh!"

Her armor had saved her from more dire wounds, but the damage had been done. She hurt, even bled. Anya chucked the broken arrows away. "She's a crafty old elven witch, I'll give her that."

"Perhaps a head-on assault is best," Cinder suggested. "We can go at them horn to horn."

Anya drew her Sky Blade. The metal sang like a tuning fork as it slipped from the sheath. She glanced down. A misty cloud formed from Fog's breath, hiding his body and the Risker.

"I can't believe I'm going to say this," she said, "but I'm not ready to rush down there and kill her yet. What do you know about Fog?"

"He's older than me. Full of tricks. A dirty old serpent, that is what he is." Cinder lowered his head and his great twisted horns. "True to his namesake, he hides himself in a fog that only he can see through. The longer we wait, the faster it will spread, and it will be harder to get at him."

Anya growled from deep within her throat. She'd never been one to fear blindly charging into battle, but in Merza's case, she hesitated.

Another arrow burst out of the mist and bore down on their position. Its head was charged with yellow fire. It whistled by overhead, stopped in midair, flipped point down, then hovered.

"How is she doing that?" Anya asked.

The arrow shot downward as if it had been fired again.

"Watch out!" She pulled Cinder's reins to the left.

Thuk! The arrow sunk into the flesh of Cinder's neck, wedging itself between the scales.

"Bloody witch! Are you hurt, Cinder?"

"No, but I felt that one. Leaves a burning sensation. Pull it out."

Anya reached over the saddle, and with two hands, she

yanked it out. Blood sizzled on the tip of the still-burning arrow. "A nasty trick," she said with disgust. "The magic still thrives."

The cloud around Fog continued to increase in size as he pursued them.

She narrowed her eyes. There was no sign of the Risker in the haze. "They can see us coming, but we can't see them."

Another arrow blasted out of the mist. It did a full loop around Cinder then sliced through the membranes of both his wings.

"Now it's getting personal," he said in more roar than voice. "What course of action, Anya?"

She yelled back, her voice full of frustration, "I don't know!"

3

Dyphestive gripped the grand dragon Rock's reins in one hand and lifted the Iron Sword high in the other. The huge black dragon burgeoning with scaled muscles thundered down the rough landscape, leaving a cloud of dust and busted stone in his wake.

In a strong and rugged voice, Rock called, "Hold tight, human! If you fall off, I won't come back for you!"

Dyphestive set his gaze on the field full of the enemies ahead. The ground was thick with dragons, grand and middling, bracing for the charge. In the center of the group was Commander Azzark. The Risker sat coolly in his saddle, sword in hand. The man's eyes switched between the battle above and the one beginning on the ground. He shouted a command, and two middling dragons and their riders launched themselves into the sky.

Commander Azzark turned his attention to Dyphestive. He pointed at them with his sword.

A pair of middling dragons came forward. The Riskers let loose a volley of arrows.

Dyphestive hunkered down over the saddle as arrows bounced off of Rock's snout and horns.

"Ha! Those needles won't hurt me!" Rock boasted.

Something about the confident look in Commander Azzark's eyes caught Dyphestive's eye. The seasoned Risker would have a trick up his sleeve, and his grand dragon would too. Unlike Rock, who was, for the most part, not very experienced in battle.

"They're baiting us," Dyphestive warned.

"Let them bait us! Rock fears nothing!" The dragon charged toward the base of the hill, stretched out his wings, then leaped. "Hang on!"

Dyphestive tightened his grip on the reins.

Rock glided toward the enemy. "I'm going for the leader. No fear!"

Commander Azzark didn't bat an eyelash.

Gliding above the surface, Rock soared over the guardian Riskers. His jaws opened wide and a stifling roar followed.

Gaze set on Commander Azzark and blood charging through his veins, Dyphestive braced himself for the collision. "It's thunder time!"

Rock sailed straight into Commander Azzark and his dragon. Except the enemy wasn't there. They'd vanished. Rock hit the ground full force and crashed into the dry landscape. He skidded across the ground, plowing up the dirt with his face.

Dyphestive fell out of the saddle with his arm twisted up in the reins. His feet dangled inches from the ground. "Horseshoes."

A cloud of dust formed around them, obscuring their vision.

"Rock, are you injured?"

The dragon snorted and shook his head. "My ego, maybe. Where'd those cowards go?"

The wind picked up, carrying the dust away. Once the smoke cleared, they were surrounded by the enemy.

Rock pulled his scaly chin out of the ground then looked around. Commander Azzark and his dragon had displaced themselves from one spot to the other. "How'd they do that?"

"I think we are in too deep to try to figure that out now." Dyphestive tugged on the reins wrapped around his hand, his feet dangling. He stretched the leather until his toes touched the ground, but the reins held fast.

"What are you gawking at, Riskers?" Commander Azzark said. "Fire on the miscreant while his chest is exposed."

From the back of a middling dragon, the nearest Risker pulled back his arrow and took aim.

Rock twisted his body around, shielding Dyphestive as the bowstring snapped.

The missile sank between the scales of Rock's neck.

"You're going to wish you didn't do that." Rock breathed out a mouthful of flame at Dyphestive's attackers, smothering them in fire.

As Rock turned, Dyphestive found himself facing a

lizardman Risker in a middling's saddle. The lizardman loaded his bow.

Breaking the leather on his wrist wasn't as easy as snapping chains. The leather stretched. Dyphestive tossed the Iron Sword point first at the ground, snuck a knife out of his belt, then started sawing the cords. Out of the corner of his eye, he watched the lizardman fire. Dyphestive turned his shoulder into it.

The burning missile sunk deep into the muscle of his upper arm. "Gargh! That stings." He sawed away at the leather, still using his wounded arm. At last, the cords snapped. He landed fully on the ground, glared at his attacker, and ripped the arrow from his shoulder.

"Big mistake." He plucked his sword from the ground and advanced at a quick pace.

A mouthful of fire came from the dragon's mouth just as Dyphestive swung and made contact.

The blood-red gemstone in the cross guard of the Iron Sword flashed. The middling dragon's body exploded into ash.

The lizardman rider dropped to the ground with his slitted eyes going as round as stones. He fumbled for his sword and pulled the blade free. Dyphestive pinned him to the ground through the chest before the Risker made it to his feet.

Dyphestive twisted his head over his shoulder and saw the whites of Commander Azzark's eyes. He and his dragon were backing away.

"Going somewhere?"

Commander Azzark's dragon beat his wings. His powerful

back legs bunched up beneath his body, and he launched himself into the sky.

"Goose eggs! He's running." He turned around and spotted Rock. The burly dragon had pinned a Risker and a middling dragon underneath his great claws. Dyphestive let out a howl. "Get 'em, brother! But make it quick. We need to get after Commander Azzark!"

Rock's massive form stood over his opponents as waves of dragon fire spewed out of his jaws, burning both man and dragon to a crisp. The Risker's body became a dried husk. The meat of the dragon's flesh shriveled underneath its scales. They were no match for Rock's raw power.

Dyphestive whacked the dragon on the backside with the flat of his sword.

Rock whipped his head around, the heat of battle churning in his eyes. "How dare you?"

"Pay attention!" He pointed at Commander Azzark flying away in the sky. "They are getting away!"

Rock huffed flames out of his nostrils. "Get on!"

4

"Are you well back there?" Fenora asked.

"I think so." Zora's knuckles were white from her tight grip on the reins. Fenora, a gorgeous grand dragon with light-jade scales splashed all over, made the long flight as gentle as possible. However, the easy part had come to an end. They flew straight into a full-fledged battle.

"How are you holding up?" Zora asked.

The sassy girl turned her head to the side and grinned with a mouthful of huge teeth. "I couldn't be more excited.

Zora nodded. She was decked out in a full suit of dragon armor that was neither comfortable nor uncomfortable at the same time, but it was hot. If not for the wind, she'd have burnt up.

Joining her to the left, Reginald the Razor rode on Slick, a middling dragon with silver scales spotting his body. Like her,

Razor was decked out in full armor. He wore an open-faced dragon helmet with wings on the side. He turned and offered her a handsome smile.

To the right, Gorva rode on a huge boy grand named Snags. The bulky all-gray dragon had a pair of tremendous teeth that jutted up from his lower jaw. One tooth was shorter than the other. Gorva, the orcen natural, sat tall in the saddle without a stitch of armor on. She'd chosen to remain in a buckskin top and bottom. She held two javelins, which flickered with energy in the palms of her large hands.

Zora took a deep breath. She didn't wear a helmet, either, but she had one in case someone else needed it. The Helm of the Dragons was tucked away in a sack tethered to the dragon's saddle. She eyed the sack. She didn't plan on wearing the artifact herself—the one time she had, it had nearly destroyed her mind. *I'd rather fight than put that thing on again.*

"I can feel your heart racing," Fenora said. "Don't worry. I'll do most of the heavy lifting, but you might want to grab a javelin. At least look like you're fighting."

"Oh." Zora absentmindedly reached back into the oversized quiver and grabbed the polished surface of the javelin. Her fingers tingled the moment she touched it. Light passed through the weapon from top to bottom like sunlight illuminating a shard of glass.

Back in Safe Haven, all of the weapons had been fully charged. The dragon allies were loaded up with additional weapons and gear. The harnesses had extra plates of armor in them for protection. They were enchanted for speed and endurance too. Bellarose, a female grand, and Chubbs, a male dragon, brought up the rear of the thunder of dragons. Like pack mules, they carried more shields, swords, axes, javelins, and other assortments of weapons.

A trio of Risker dragons came right at them. The riders stood up in the stirrups and fired arrows that streaked through the sky like burning firefly tails.

"Here comes the welcoming committee!" Fenora said.

Gorva and Snags flew head-on into the assault. An arrow clacked off the brutish dragon's skull. Razor and Slick veered right, easing away from a deadly missile. Fenora swooped under an arrow.

"We'll take the leader!" Fenora slipped beneath the lead dragon, a grand checkered with white scales.

Zora hurled her javelin at the beast's white belly. The weapon flew out of her hand like a bolt of lightning. It whizzed by the dragon and missed by several yards.

"Well, that was awful."

"You have to time it better," Fenora said. "Anticipate. But hang on tight!" Her wings pumped, and she did a loop midair back toward the enemy.

"Ahhh!" Zora's hair hung upside down, and she saw nothing but the ground passing below her. Her feet in the stirrups kept her from plummeting to certain death.

Fenora made a corkscrew twist and came upright again. They were behind the Risker and chasing its tail.

As Zora's stomach bounced back into place, she muttered, "I think I'm going to be sick." She reached back and grabbed another javelin. An arrow whistled over her head. "Dirty chipmunks, that was close!"

"You have to keep your head down below my horns. That Risker has good aim." Fenora flew after the dragon as it tried to shake her, its flight erratic. "Fast dragon, too, but I'll catch it! Once I get that tail, go for it with a javelin. Hopefully, you won't miss at close range."

"What's that supposed to mean?"

"You need practice."

Zora hunkered down in the saddle, javelin in hand, as she was slung from side to side by the chase. The dragons moved like great birds in the sky, shifting, twisting, and dodging through the air.

Fenora nipped at the enemy dragon's tail, but it veered downward and away. She overshot the mark, twisted into a dive, then closed in again.

"Whew! If it wasn't for this harness, my wings would have fallen off by now!" she said above the rushing wind. "Listen to me—I won't miss this time. Be ready!"

"I will!" With the wind tearing through her hair, Zora squeezed the javelin and hefted it on her shoulder. She locked her eyes on the Risker.

Fenora closed the gap. Jaws wide, she made her move. The enemy dragon zigzagged left then back to the right. She anticipated the move, flew right, then closed her jaws into the meaty middle of the dragon's tail.

The enemy dragon roared. The Risker, a strapping human, turned in his saddle and fired an arrow into Fenora's skull.

"No!" Zora let the javelin fly. It shot out of her hand like a crossbow bolt and blasted through the Risker's chest armor. The man clutched the huge wound and fell out of the saddle.

Fenora's jaws loosened on the dragon's tail. She glided toward the ground in a slow, lazy circle.

Zora called out to her. "Fenora! Fenora! What's wrong?"

The dragon didn't answer.

5

Razor and Slick tangled in the sky with a Risker and his middling dragon. Talons raked over scales, and both dragons butted horns with a clack.

"Take this fight to the ground before I fall out of this saddle!" Razor fought to put his foot back into the stirrup. "Bloody blades! I'm slipping!" He clutched the saddle horn with two hands.

Out of the corner of his eye, he caught the Risker fighting to keep his aim on Slick as the dragons jerked around in the sky. Razor eyed a javelin, reached one arm out, and grabbed it. He thrust it underneath the enemy dragon's wing, and it sank several inches deep.

The dragon's roar turned into a shriek. It twisted out of Slick's claws.

"Got him!" Razor grinned and thumped his chest.

"Well done, but I had him," Slick coolly replied. "It looks like they are going to the ground. You'll get your wish."

Razor watched the Risker guide his mount toward the hot plains. The dragon quavered, hit the ground feet first, then stumbled into the dirt.

"Ha! I didn't get him that good."

The Risker hopped out of the saddle, stood by his dragon, and drew two swords. He beckoned Razor to him.

"Take us down! This one wants a real fight!" Razor laughed in his roguish manner. "And he'll have it!"

Slick opened his wings and made a soft landing a few dozen yards from the enemy. The wind blew dust in their eyes, and he shielded Razor with his wing. "All right, you take the dragon, and I'll take the sword swinger."

Razor gave Slick an incredulous look. "No, it's the other way around. He challenged me, not you."

"I think he was challenging *me*."

"No, me!" Razor fired back. He ran out from behind the dragon's wing and charged across the blistering sand. He picked up speed and went straight for the Risker.

"Hey!" Slick yelled from behind.

The Risker's eyes widened as Razor approached. He was well-knit, like the others of his ilk, and wore a beard and finely crafted black armor. The Risker moved into a fighting stance, keeping his back to the wind.

Smart move, Razor thought as he drew his own blades. He'd been itching to battle with the Sky Blades he'd acquired in the

Safe Haven's armory. The long swords were perfectly balanced and fit his hand like a glove. "It won't do you any good."

The Risker sank further into his stance. At the last moment, he lunged.

Razor batted the warrior's first sword aside with a flick of his wrist. He caught the man's other blade on his cross guard. They locked up, nose to nose, driving chest against chest.

"Any last words?" Razor asked.

"Die!" The Risker shoved him back then lunged again. Flashing metal rang against metal in a cadence of death.

Steel whistled over Razor's head as he crouched down. The blade clipped the top of his helmet, sending it off-kilter. He danced back and slung the helmet off. "The Flaming Fence on that thing. It's going to get me killed."

The Risker pressed the attack, swinging high and low.

Razor parried both blades and stayed on the defensive. But his mouth went on the offensive as he worked his skill. "Before you die, I think it's only fair that you know my name. Perhaps you've heard of me? I'm Reginald the Razor."

With his arms pumping sharp steel toward Razor's chest, the man answered, "A laughable name. I'm Hile Gurst. I let my blades, not silly names, speak for me."

He snaked one blade through Razor's defenses and sliced him across the upper arm. "First blood!"

"That's not even a scratch. A fine effort, but you've exposed yourself, haven't you?" Razor casually parried blow after blow. "But this time, I've seen your best attacks. I've noticed your weaknesses too."

He blocked the man's incoming swing. "Your footwork is good, but far from perfection. You drop your elbows a moment before you attack."

"So you say!" Hile Gurst showed red beneath his hairy cheeks. "I've shown you nothing." He thrust with both blades.

Razor spun away from the attack and swatted the man on his backside. "A shame really. A few months of training with me, and you could have been an outstanding swordsman. Not such as yours truly, but better than most."

"Shut your mouth!" Laboring for breath, Hile Gurst turned and attacked again.

"But I'm not finished speaking." Razor blocked both blades to opposite sides. He counter-attacked and plunged both swords deep into the man's chest. "As I said, Hile Gurst, I am Reginald the Razor. I defeated you."

The Risker choked, fell backward, then landed flat on his back with both swords still gripped in his hands.

Razor wiped his blades clean with a cloth he kept in his armor then sheathed his weapons.

Slick was nearby, caring for the wounded dragon.

"What do we have here?" Razor said. "You didn't kill it?"

"No. It's a she, and she surrendered." Slick stroked the enemy dragon's wing. "You clipped her good, but she'll make it."

"But won't she attack us?"

"No, you killed her master. She has free will unless they take her again, and we won't let that happen."

Razor nodded and studied the sky. "If you say so." He sheathed his swords. "The ranks of our enemy are thinning. I'm not used to that." He slowly turned all the way around. "We better keep moving. Somebody somewhere is going to need our help."

Slick nodded. He petted the balled-up dragon, her wings folded on her back and her tail curled around her body. "We'll be back."

Slick moved toward Razor. "Get on."

Razor climbed into the saddle. "Ride the sky!"

6

The sons and daughters of Cinder were an agile group. Snags, despite his brutish build, was no exception. He chased after the Risker riding on a middling dragon, but the smaller zigzagging dragon proved too quick to accurately follow.

"What's the matter? Can't you keep up?" Gorva beat her fist on a round buckler she used. Two arrows were stuck in the metal. "At least get close enough for me to get a shot at them."

"Be patient," Snags said in a low and grumbling voice. "I've been flying day and night."

"Excuses, excuses!" Gorva patted him on the flat spot behind his horns. "We'll get them. I want to take that Risker down. Did you see how he sneered at me?"

"I did."

The Risker turned in his saddle and took aim again. He was an immense half orc with long braids hanging over his back. His armor was packed tightly over bulging chest muscles, his huge biceps bare. He was as big as Dyphestive, if not bigger. He pulled the bowstring back along his cheek, made another ugly grin, then fired.

The missile streaked through the air like a burning hornet. It punched one more hole in the shield in front of Gorva's face.

"Anvils!" the orcen woman said. "He has quite the aim for a thick-thewed man." She noticed the dragon charm mounted into the Risker's breastplate. "Be wary. He's a natural. He'll have more than one trick up his sleeve."

The middling dragon dove, barrel-rolled, and started into a loop underneath Snags.

"Hang tight!" Snags thrust upward, going into his own upward circle.

Both dragons went high and low then flew back into each other's path on a full collision course.

"Perfect!" Snags opened his jaws and sprayed bright-orange fire.

The Risker's dragon dipped underneath the flames, below Snags's belly. The half orc fired an arrow in Snags's gut at the same time.

"Gurk!" Snags shuddered, his fire breath cut short. His beating wings quivered.

"Snags, are you wounded?" Gorva rose in the stirrups toward his head.

He straightened his flight pattern. "Nothing I can't handle." He made a raspy sigh. His beating wings slowed.

Gorva knew at that moment that the wound was serious. The Risker had found a weak spot in Snags's armor and hit it.

They're going to carve us up if I don't end this soon.

She leaned toward Snags's earhole and said, "You need to land. Otherwise, they'll pick us to death!"

"I'm fine!"

"I know you are, but they don't need to know that. Act more wounded than you are!"

"What?"

"I know you are hurting but make them think your wound is graver than it is. We need to fake a crash landing. Let them think they've won."

"Playing possum isn't my style."

"It isn't mine either. But what choice do we have?"

Snags grumbled. "Brace yourself. I can't make it look easy."

"I'm ready."

One of Snags's wings stopped beating. With the other, he made a controlled glide and spiraled downward.

Above, the Risker waved and showed a triumphant smile. At the same time, he nocked another arrow in his bow.

He's not going to let up, Gorva thought. *Merciless. I admire that.* She raised her buckler. A moment later, an arrow blasted into it. *Thuk!*

The head of the enchanted arrow protruded from the shield, and the others embedded there pulsed like a heartbeat.

"What is this all about?" The hairs on the nape of Gorva's neck stood up. "Snags, watch out!" She flung the buckler away.

Boom! The explosion's concussive force knocked Gorva over

the side of Snags's saddle. Sharp chunks from the metal buckler sank into the skin of her arms and chest. Spots formed in her eyes. Grabbing the saddle horn, she straightened herself.

"Slute!" she cursed. Dazed, half-blinded, and shieldless, she was a sitting duck. "We need to fake this accident quickly."

"Bear with me. It's my first time causing my own accident." Snags dropped faster, and his flight became more out of control.

Gorva clung to the reins in one hand and rubbed her eyes with the fist of the other. She blinked repeatably. The bright flash from the explosion had seared her cheeks. Her obscured vision began to clear. Shielding her eyes from the sun, she looked about. There was no sign of the Risker.

"Where are you?"

"Brace yourself. We're moments from kissing the dirt," Snags said.

She rose in her saddle and saw the barren plains waiting to greet them. She crouched down into the saddle.

Thud! Snags skidded across the ground then came to a sudden halt. The stirred-up dust covered them like a blanket.

Coughing, Gorva grabbed a battle-ax and dropped from Snags's big body. "Make it look like you landed on me," she whispered. "Pinned more down."

Snags shifted his frame up. At the same time, he scooped away a shallow grave in the dirt. "Get in there."

Gorva concealed the battle-ax in the pile of dirt and crawled into the pocket. The grand dragon lowered on top of her, and she lay with her hips buried under the dragon.

The hot winds from the arid climate chased the cloud of dust away. Nearby, the Risker landed. He jumped from the saddle and swept his braids back over his shoulder. He carried a spiked mace with a round head in his grip. His long strides carried his big frame across the short distance in a matter of seconds. He stopped a few yards away.

"I see you breathing," the Risker said. "Impressive. My enemies don't live so long."

Gorva faked trying to claw her way out from underneath the dragon and grunted. "Guh!"

The half orc gave a rugged laugh and squatted down. "You really are a fighter. An attractive one too." He titled his head. "What is your name, woman?"

She fought to get the words out. "None of your business."

"I am Ruddukk the Slayer." His dark beady eyes narrowed, and his eyebrows knitted together. "You know me?"

Gorva gritted her teeth and her blood began to rise. She did know him. "I do."

Ruddukk removed his helmet, fully revealing his ugly and pitted face. "How so?"

Gorva pushed up from her chest, spit on the ground, then screamed, "Because you're the dog that killed my mother!"

7

Gorva hadn't been fully grown when it'd happened. The youngest of many siblings, she was the lone survivor and had been condemned to Prisoner Island.

The Riskers had come like thieves in the night, striking a remote village near Harbor Lake. They'd come on orders to hunt down any surviving members of the Sky Riders' families. Dragons turned the small establishment to flames. The people fled. The family of Gorva's father, Hogrim, fought to the bitter end.

Among the Riskers was their leader. Gorva had never gotten a good look at the man, but she remembered his name. Ruddukk the Slayer. He'd personally killed her mother, Marva, and a brother and sister as well.

Why Gorva hadn't been slain, she didn't know. Perhaps she'd been too young to kill, or perhaps they'd slipped. One way or the other, sending her to Prisoner Island had been as good as a death sentence. But the daughter of Hogrim had survived. She'd learned to thrive.

The day had come when her family would be avenged.

"Your mother?" Ruddukk raised an eyebrow. "I don't recall. After all, I've killed so many, hence the name *Slayer*. Perhaps you can be more specific." He tapped his temple with his finger. "I have a very keen memory of all my kills."

"My mother's name was Marva."

He shrugged. "As I said, there are so many. I don't remember the names sometimes, but I never forget the event."

"You'll remember her name forever after today." Her nostrils flared. "She was the wife of Hogrim the Sky Rider, my father."

Ruddukk's mouth dropped open slightly. "Is that so? I'm not sure how you survived, but as with most of my duties, it's up to me to fully execute the task at hand.

"Daughter of Hogrim the Sky Rider"—he lifted his mace high and charged—"say hello to the kiss of death!"

On her elbows, Gorva wormed her way out from underneath Snags and grabbed her battle-ax out of the sand. She rose to one knee and blocked.

Spiked mace crashed against ax. *Clang!*

The painful, jarring impact carried through her arms into her shoulders. Weapons locked up, and she pushed back against Ruddukk's might.

"You are strong, woman, but not stronger than me."

"I am today!" Gorva stuffed her boot in his gut.

He stumbled several yards from the kick and backpedaled to

a stop. His face turned into an angry smile. "You'll regret you ever crossed me!" The spikes on his mace turned into flame. His eyes matched the fire. Muscles heaved beneath his armor, and his leather buckles stretched. "There will be nothing left of you when I'm finished."

"We'll see about that!" Gorva charged. She'd never learned to master her own wizard fire. It was too late to learn then. Revenge would be her flame. "Taste my steel!"

Before she made it to him, Ruddukk swung what seemed much too early. She hadn't even been close. Then the head of his mace popped off, connected by a line of chain.

She flattened on the ground, ducking under the ball and chain that whizzed over her face. She watched the head of the mace snap back into place.

"You'll never get close!" Ruddukk flicked his weapon at her again, and the flaming ball careened toward her.

She jumped away like a frog and landed far away. "Coward!"

He wagged his finger at her. "No. Only smart. If you wish, you can always surrender."

"Never, you murderer!" She stormed in at full speed.

The ball of flaming spikes shot straight toward her. Gorva cocked back her ax and clubbed the flaming head aside. She kept charging.

"No!" a wide-eyed Ruddukk croaked. "You can't do—"

Gorva's backswing cleaved through the half orc's neck. The enemy gurgled as Ruddukk's head rolled off of his shoulders. His body collapsed in the bloody sand beside it.

The head of the mace retracted, and the flame went out. She kicked it out of his hand and exhaled.

From the corner of her eye, the middling dragon attacked. Snags came out of nowhere, horns first, and plowed into the middling's wings and ribs.

The middling squared off with the grand, spread out its wings, and spit out a stream of fire. Snags unleashed his own fiery breath. Plumes of fire kissed and blossomed out.

Gorva backed away, shielding her face from the scorching heat.

The bigger dragon backed the smaller one down. His flames consumed the others. Dragon fire seared scales. The middling shrieked one last cry, spasmed fiercely, and succumbed to the flames and suffocating heat. Snags tore into the charred body with his teeth and claws. A dragon's burned wing came off. The job was finished.

Snags huffed out one last ball of fire and roared. He swung his head around on his thick neck to Gorva. "Revenge, huh? Feel better?"

"Better than I have in a long time." She bent over and picked up Ruddukk's mace. She tossed it up, flipping it end over, and caught it. "And it has its rewards."

Snags approached and raised his wing, revealing the arrow buried between his belly scales. "Would you be so kind and take care of this? A handsbreadth to the left, and it might have done permanent damage to my wing."

She grabbed the arrow just below the feathers. "Fast or slow?"

"Slow—"

Gorva ripped it out.

"Ouch." He casually flapped his wing. "Apparently, your definition of slow has a different meaning."

She patted him on his largest snaggle tooth. "You'll live."

8

Cinder faced the expanding cloud as he flew backward.

"Careful, brother," Anya said. "You're leaving your chest exposed. Merza's arrows are impossible to stop." She kept her eyes peeled, waiting for another one of the deadly missiles to blast out of the mist. "They can see us, but we can't see them."

"As I've stated, this isn't the first time I've tangled with Fog. Do you trust me?"

"Of course I do."

Cinder nodded. He set his gaze on the cloud. "Good, because we are going in. Trust your instincts. We'll probably only have one chance at this." His wings beat as he turned his back and increased his distance from the cloud.

Anya grabbed her Sky Blade's handle and pulled it from the sheath. She had a general idea of what Cinder was about to do. If the dragon could hear the enemy, smell them out, they'd have a target. Stoking her energy within, she prepared to call her lightning strike.

They flew below the sky's cloud cover, but the ever-growing cloud that Merza and Fog had created pursued close behind. Cinder picked up speed and jettisoned underneath the cotton-like bed of clouds.

Anya swore that she heard a wicked chuckle as she spotted Merza's ghostly face form in the mist. A radiant arrow shot out of the apparition's mouth.

"Incoming!" she shouted, but Cinder made a beeline for the missile. "Dodge, Cinder!"

The dragon didn't veer from his path. He hit the arrow head-on. It buried deep inside his snout, but he kept going. He followed the arrow's trajectory, and they plunged into the mist.

Anya lost sight of everything. She'd flown through clouds before, but they were nothing like the mist. If she didn't feel Cinder underneath her, she wouldn't even know he was there. Cinder's wings no longer beat. They sailed through stark whiteness.

This is insane! Where is that dragon witch?

Thuk! Thuk! Arrows buried themselves in Cinder's body.

Thuk! A third struck Anya's thigh. She groaned. "I am sick of this!"

Cinder twisted into the path where the arrows had come from, but the way they bent in the sky made it impossible to track their origin. He huffed out a stream of fire, and the flames ate up the mist.

The dragon breath gave Anya a brief glimpse of the white

field within. But another arrow struck Cinder in the face, cutting off his flame off. Still, she knew she'd seen some movement in the cloud. Her eyes flickered like shimmering stars.

Anya called forth her lightning. "Thunderbolts from the heavens, seek out my enemies! Come!"

It was no ordinary lightning strike. The air rumbled. A bright streak flashed and splintered through the mist. Cords of lightning came down like rain and smote the spot where Anya took aim. The slivers of silver light passed through the mist, lighting up the gloom and vanishing again.

"Anvils!" Anya cursed.

Cinder sniffed. "No, wait. Do you smell that?"

There was no mistaking the smell of charred flesh and scale. Anya didn't see the strike, but she'd hit something.

"I have them now!" Cinder veered toward the scent, powerful wings pumping.

Two more arrows struck. *Thuk! Thuk!*

Through the whiteness of the cloud, Anya heard Merza cry out. "Nooo!"

Cinder rammed Fog at full speed. Horn met horn like a thunderclap. *Clack!*

Anya clung to the saddle, and her helmet shifted over her eyes. She pushed it back into place. There Merza was, her white hair a tangled mess and the white fog dissipating all around.

The spell was broken. The fight was on.

"Clever! But you are no match for me, child!" Merza's elegant fingers massaged the air as she shouted. "Suffocate on your brief victory!"

Anya lost her breath and gagged. The air had simply been taken from her lungs. She clutched at her throat with one hand.

Cinder and Fog were locked up, chest to chest, wings beating furiously as they dropped through the sky. Talons ripped open scale and flesh. Flames shot from their nostrils.

Gloating in her saddle, Merza crossed her arms with a triumphant look on her beautiful elven face. She flipped her silky white hair over her shoulder. "Don't worry, dear. It will be over soon."

Yes, it will. Breathless, Anya summoned every ounce of wizard fire she could from the depths of her gut. The Sky Blade shimmered. The air around them popped.

Merza's lovely eyes grew like saucers. Her face whipped up to the sky.

Lightning came straight down. A cord of shining rope struck Merza full in the face and blasted its way through her body and into Fog's. The elf's skeleton lit up beneath her skin. Her lustrous hair rolled up to her shoulders and turned black.

Gasping, Anya caught her breath. She swayed in her seat and clung to the reins.

Cinder's jaws latched around Fog's throat. He shook the dragon's neck, biting down until the bone made a loud snap. Once it did, he let the monstrous winged beast fall.

Anya leaned over the saddle, panting, and watched her enemy plummet toward the earth.

In a spasm, Fog twisted over Merza. He landed on top of her as they splattered against the rocky ground.

"Are you wounded?" Anya reached for Cinder and stroked the scales beneath his horns.

"Merely scratches. You?"

"After I dig these arrowheads out of me, I'll be fine." She sat up in the saddle and took a deep breath. "Let's help the others. Ride the sky, Cinder! Ride the sky!"

9

Commander Azzark retreated at full speed.

Rock's wings labored, but the fifty-yard gap between them did not lessen. Azzark's dragon headed north and stretched the lead.

"He's going after reinforcements." Dyphestive stood up on his stirrups. "We have to catch him."

"I'm trying," Rock growled. "Even with this harness, my wings tire."

A shadow passed over them. Grey Cloak and Streak were flying above him. The elf waved, and Streak dropped down beside Rock.

"How's it going, brother?" Grey Cloak shouted above the wind.

Dyphestive pointed at Commander Azzark. "He's getting away!"

Streak shook his head. "Nah, he's not going anywhere." His twin tails kicked behind him. "We'll get him." He scooted ahead.

"No, wait!" Dyphestive shouted. "He uses displacement. Where he appears, he isn't!"

"One way or the other, we'll get him." Grey Cloak glanced back behind them and gave a quick nod.

Dyphestive turned in the saddle. "Kiss my boots!"

A thunder of dragons flew at their rear—the children of Cinder and their riders, members of Talon.

"What about the enemy?" Dyphestive called.

Grey Cloak smirked. "I can't believe I'm saying this, but we defeated them—one and all!"

"You mean, there is only one left?" Dyphestive started to smile.

"We haven't seen any other threats. I know how you feel. I've had to pinch myself more than once." Grey Cloak raised his arm and motioned forward.

Slicer, a sleek middling with impressive razor-sharp claws, sped ahead. He was followed by Slick and Razor. The middling Feather, splashed with pink scales, was right on Slick's tail.

"Commander Azzark won't outrun us," Grey Cloak said. "We'll cut him off and send him back your way." Grey Cloak rose in his stirrups. "See you soon, brother!"

Dyphestive saluted.

Rock growled. "The little ones are going to have all the fun. I don't like it."

"We'll manage." Behind him, Dyphestive could see the rest of the dragons—all grands, aside from Chubbs and Bellarose, who hadn't appeared. He caught Zora waving at him from Fenora's back and waved in return.

Zora and Gorva flew on Snags and caught up to Rock and flanked his sides.

"It's good to see you, Dyphestive," Gorva said.

"You too!"

Ahead, the middling dragons caught up with Commander Azzark, forcing the Risker and his grand to turn back. Grey Cloak used the Rod of Weapons and fired balls of energy at the Risker, but the bright orbs of light passed harmlessly through him. The man and dragon blinked from one spot to another and then multiplied from one dragon rider into three.

"Kiss my boots!" Zora said. "Which one is it?"

"He can only be one of them! I'll take the one in the middle!" Dyphestive shouted.

"Now this is my kind of fight!" A surge of energy sped up Rock's wings. He nosed in front of the pack. "Full speed ahead!"

Anya and Cinder appeared out of nowhere and blasted straight into the middle dragon, knocking the enemy sideways in the sky in a thunderous collision.

The other two versions of Commander Azzark vanished.

"Father, no! That was my fight!" Rock yelled.

Cinder gripped Commander Azzark in his talons and squeezed. The Risker's eyes bulged in their sockets. A loud crack and pop of metal followed.

Rock, Fenora, and Snags drove the Risker's dragon from the sky. They bit and clawed apart the evil dragon's wings then chased it to the ground. The moment the dragons crashed into the plains, Dyphestive, Zora, and Gorva bailed off their saddles. Cinder's three children pounced on the enemy dragon and tore it to pieces.

Commander Azzark's wrecked body landed behind them, creating a cloud of dust and leaving an impression in the land. When the dirty smoke cleared, the Risker still breathed, but his final breath came quickly.

Zora leaned over with her hands on her knees and caught her breath. "Is it over? Tell me it's over."

Dyphestive looked around. "I think so." He moved over to Zora and put his hand on her back. "Are you sick?"

"Queasy but happy to be alive." She straightened and threw her arms around his waist. "Lords of the Sky, it's good to see you!"

He mussed her short hair with his hand, which swallowed half of her head. "Glad you made it."

GREY CLOAK and Streak landed near Dyphestive. They were joined by Slick, Razor, and Slicer.

The rest of the thunder of dragons landed, including Anya and Cinder. All of the riders dismounted and joined together.

Anya removed her helmet and gave a fierce smile. "The battle is won. A good one!"

"I find it hard to believe, but we've searched for more threats, and we haven't found any." Grey Cloak looked over his shoulder, south, toward Dwarf Skull. "I probably shouldn't say it, but I think we can breathe easy for now."

"Look!" Dyphestive pointed toward the sky. "More dragons!"

Two grand dragons approached from the east. They flew in a slow and lazy pattern.

Streak stretched up his neck, squinting. "Hey, that's only Chubby and Bellarose. They finally made it." He released a plume of fire.

The heavyset dragons came their way. Both of them made a rough landing and panted with their tongues lolling out. They didn't have riders, but they were loaded down with enough weapons and armor to start a small army.

Chubby had big brown eyes like a puppy, and he spoke in a slow, friendly voice. "Where can a dragon get some water? I'm dying of thirst."

Bellarose had the pretty pattern of lavender scales splashed over her body. The burly girl dragon spoke with a husky voice. She yawned and said, "Where's the fight?"

"It's over," Streak said.

"Over?" Bellarose yawned again. "We carried all of this stuff for nothing?" She shook her head. "I'm going to sleep."

"Let's get a drink first and find a shady spot." Chubby gave a disappointed shake of his skull, nudged his sister, and wandered away.

"Now what?" Dyphestive asked his brother.

"We still have to find Chopper. Crazy little sand gnome stole the Stone of Transport. Without it, we can't build the Apparatus of Ruune." He swept his cloak behind his shoulders. "We need to form a search party. If we sniff out Tiny, we should be able to find Chopper."

Zanna Paydark, Lythlenion, Shannon, Crane, and Queen Rhonna with her four dwarves approached from the south.

"Well, that was one dwarf of a fight," Rhonna said. Without cracking a smile, she added, "I'm proud of you boys."

Grey Cloak's throat swelled up. "Thanks," he said. "With the Riskers gone, is Dwarf Skull free?"

Rhonna managed a sliver of a smile. "I have no doubt that the Black Guard are overcome by now. But there's only one way to know for sure. Let's go take a look."

10

DWARF SKULL

The streets of Dwarf Skull filled with excitement as the dead bodies of the Black Guard were hauled out of the city. Surviving members of the wicked troops were imprisoned in the Hold. With their enemy gone, the great city was in full celebration. Boarded-up shops were opened, and keg barrels of dwarven ale were tapped. The dwarves belted out raucous songs of victory, sang praises to their queen, and danced with vigor, elbows swinging, on their stubby booted feet.

Dyphestive and a few members of Talon—Lythlenion, Razor, Crane, Shannon, and Gorva—accompanied Queen Rhonna with her four dwarfsmen. As the queen led the way down the streets, the dwarves in the crowd bowed and took a knee as she passed.

"Hail to the queen!" a gusty dwarf said. "Hail to Queen Rhonna! She brings us victory!"

The dwarves waved their weapons in the air and let out a chorus of robust cheers.

"Hail Queen Rhonna! Hail Queen Rhonna! Hail Queen Rhonna!"

"They really adore you here, don't they?" Dyphestive said.

Rhonna waved at her subject and said out of the corner of her mouth, "Don't say that. It's embarrassing. I'm a farmer, nothing more, nothing less."

"No, you're far more than that. Perhaps that is why they are so fond of you." Dyphestive reached out his hand to lay it on her shoulder. The dwarven quartet bristled. "So, where are we going?"

Rhonna carried the plans for the Apparatus of Ruune in her grip. "To the armory. Now that we've taken Dwarf Skull back, we can use all of our resources and build this contraption faster. I looked at the plans, and it's more intricate than I noticed the first time."

Crane caught up with Rhonna. He waved at the crowd with a broad smile on his face. "This is fantastic! But where are the women? I was hoping to—well, you know—meet them." He hitched his thumbs in his belt underneath his belly. "They are renowned for their hero's welcome. The feasts, massages. I could use some pampering after that battle."

"The women and children are in hiding, but they'll be brought along soon enough," she said. "Your pampering will have to wait." She waved the plans from side to side. "We have to get this built. Time is pressing, like Grey Cloak says."

"We are here to help, Rhonna—er, I mean, Queen Rhonna." Dyphestive offered a bow.

"Rhonna is fine. You aren't one of my subjects."

They continued marching through the city and were joined by a host of soldiers. They led the way to a huge pair of iron doors that stood taller than two men. The doors were boarded up.

Rhonna nodded at the soldiers. They took out pry bars and hammers and tore the boards loose in seconds. They grabbed the door handles by the rings and pulled the door open.

Dyphestive beheld the largest armory he'd ever seen. Even the Vault in Safe Haven was not as immense. There were forges aplenty, at least a score from a glance. In the darkness, the depths were endless. Great chains hung above, dangling from rafters and pulleys. Huge urns hung by every furnace.

"Dwarves, I want those fires hot," Rhonna commanded as she strode inside. "All of them. And fetch our best blacksmiths."

As their company followed Rhonna inside, a pair of dwarven soldiers started their way out.

"Hurry!" Rhonna called after them.

The dwarves picked up the pace and disappeared.

One by one, the furnaces were lit, and the coals glowed. Still, Rhonna had a grim expression.

"What's wrong?" Crane asked.

"It's going to take some time to get those furnaces hot enough to start melting. At least a day."

"I don't think we have a day." Dyphestive frowned.

"Then man those bellows. We're going to need all the wind we can muster," Rhonna said.

Dyphestive walked deeper into the giant forge and stood by one of the man-sized bellows by the furnace. He'd worked in Rhonna's armory for years and knew how long it took to get the coals burning. A smaller furnace required just hours, but those massive ones would take a lot longer. He turned toward her and smiled.

"What's that look for?"

"I know how to get these coals hot in an instant."

Rhonna crossed her arms. "How's that?"

He grinned. "Where there be fire, there be dragons."

Slick and Slicer moseyed into the armory. The sleek dragons snaked their way into the forge, sniffing the tools and tables but not touching a thing. Dyphestive guided them through the aisle of furnaces. Slick stuck his head in the mouth of one.

"Light this? No problem." His voice made a hollow echo inside. He turned toward his brother. "Let's light these candles, brother."

Slicer scraped his claws together. "My pleasure. You take this side, and I'll take the other. Race you to the finish." He sprinted across the aisles to the other side.

Furnace by furnace, each dragon unleashed a tight stream of flame. Slick turned one pile of coals into a bright orange fire and quickly moved to the next. The furnaces came to life, and the entire armory warmed like a living thing.

Some of the dwarves jumped on the tables and started making gusty cheers, egging the racing dragons on. Coins exchanged hands as the wagering began.

The dragons were neck and neck. They quickened the pace toward the finish.

Slick set the last furnace in his row aflame a hair quicker than Slicer. "Yes! I win!" He gasped for breath.

Slicer lit his then joined his brother. "Well done." He took a deep breath. "I'm hungry after that."

They wandered down the broad center aisle, wing against wing. The dwarves cheered them on with praises. They stopped in front of Rhonna.

"Can you direct us to your livestock?" Razor asked. "After all of that, we are quite famished."

Rhonna nodded to one of her soldiers. "Follow him. Eat all you want." She gazed at the armory then turned to Dyphestive. "A thing of beauty isn't it?"

He smiled.

She approached a table and rolled out the plans. "Let's get to work."

11

Streak walked the plains with his snout to the ground, sniffing. Grey Cloak walked alongside him, and Zanna and Zora were having a conversation far behind them.

Dragon shadows passed overhead. Some of the children of Cinder joined their search for Tiny the cyclops from the sky, while others rested their wings like Streak.

"You know, Tiny's scent isn't very hard to follow considering that he smells so bad," Streak commented. "Cyclops have a very distinct salty odor. Can you smell it?"

"Not really," Grey Cloak said absentmindedly. He sighed. "That little gnome could be anywhere now. Anywhere in the world. It might be impossible to find him."

"Didn't you say Tiny would know where to find him?"

"Aye. But I don't think Tiny understands the nature of the

Stone of Transport's power. It can change a person. Make life easy. Too easy."

Grey Cloak had used the stone to his advantage. Its power was addictive. Being able to travel anywhere in the world with a single thought gave him a charge that he'd never forget. With such power, there was no predicting where the sand gnome would go.

They'd been walking for the better part of a league. The wind had taken Tiny's tracks away, but the scent remained strong enough for Streak. One rocky rise after another, they moved on at a brisk pace, but time was running out.

In the back of his head, Grey Cloak knew that Black Frost was destroying the Wizard Watch towers. Gossamer, disguised at Dirklen, had managed to lead the humongous dragon north, near Dark Mountain. It had bought time, but he wasn't sure whether it was enough for the dwarves to build the Apparatus of Ruune. Without the Stone of Transport, the artifact might not have enough power to work. The questions plagued Grey Cloak's mind.

We have to find that stone. If we don't, we are doomed.

He glanced over his shoulder at Zanna and Zora, who appeared to be enjoying their conversation. Gorva had wandered up behind them. Those three were some of the strongest and most dependable people he knew. He was thankful for the odd family he'd inherited over the course of the quest. The question was whether they'd all survive. He was determined, no matter what, to make that happen.

Inside his pocket, he gripped the Figurine of Heroes. He'd

retrieved it after the battle. The strange artifact had bailed them out several times, but it gave him little comfort. He let it drop deeper into his pocket.

He looked back once more. Zora nonchalantly waved without breaking her conversation with Zanna.

"Zanna, you need to take the Helm of the Dragons." Zora dusted the sand out of her eyes. "I should have used it, but... I couldn't. I don't want to—it's too powerful, and I'm not a natural. It's meant for people like you."

"We'll see." Zanna shrugged.

"What do you mean by that?"

Zanna combed her fingers back through her silky black hair. "Sometimes, you have to do what must be done. What happens if you are the last of us left?"

"I'm sure that isn't going to happen. Will you please take it?"

Zanna stopped and planted her fists on her hips. "Look at me. I travel light. I don't have any room for a helmet."

"I travel light too. I'm a thief, you know."

Gorva caught up with them and said, "I don't like helmets either. Nor armor, for that matter. So don't ask me."

"I wasn't going to ask you."

Gorva walked on. "Yes, you were."

Zora frowned. "She's right. I was."

"Don't overthink it. When the time comes," Gorva said, "I'm sure the helm will be in the right hands."

"Hopefully, this artifact we are building will take care of that." Zora opened Crane's satchel and grabbed a small jar of salve. "Gorva! Wait. Let me treat your wounds."

"They are fine!" Gorva kept walking.

Zora offered the jar to Zanna instead. "Do you need it?"

"I need rest, but other than that, I'm well." Zanna resumed her trek. "The Helm of the Dragons is a creation of Wizard Watch. Perhaps Tatiana will take the burden off your hands."

"But she's not a natural either."

"You don't have to be a natural to use dragon charms. You know that. You've used them before. Did you have any problems then?"

"The helmet is different. You hear so many minds at once. It's impossible to control them."

"Well, if we don't find the Stone of Transport, the helm might be the only weapon we have to fend off Black Frost."

"Ugh!" Zora said. "That's what I'm trying to say. I can't try to control the likes of him or his army of dragons. You need someone stronger than me."

"I have faith in you."

Zora dropped her head and sighed. "That's not what I want to hear. Quit toying with me."

Zanna smirked. She hooked Zora's arm and walked her forward. "Stop thinking about it so much. Think about other things, like the future. Your future with my son, perhaps."

"What?"

"I know you are fond of him, and he is fond of you. I've seen how you connect." Zanna leaned into her. "I'd love to have grandchildren."

"Grandchildren?" Zora blushed.

Gorva looked back at them, as did Grey Cloak, who was farther away.

Zanna giggled. "How's *that* to keep your mind off things?"

"You're devious."

"Thank you," Zanna replied.

12

They spotted Tiny another league away. The lumpy-headed cyclops hid in the rocky cluster of hills that worked as a natural camouflage.

"Wait here," Grey Cloak told Streak and the others.

Judging by Tiny's body language—squatted down with his neck craned—he was spying on someone. Hopefully, that someone was Chopper.

Grey Cloak stole his way through the crevices that made a rough path between the stones. He made it behind Tiny. The cyclops didn't move.

"Psst!" Grey Cloak said.

Tiny turned his thick neck, held a finger to his lips, and made a silent shush. He pointed at a spot farther down the hill. There was a burrow underneath the overhanging rocks. Quietly, he said, "Chopper has a little hovel down there. It's too small for me to squeeze into."

Grey Cloak crawled up a rock and leaned over the edge. "Have you seen him?"

Tiny shook his head. "No." His nostrils flared. "But I smelled him. He's in there. That's where he goes. He calls it his lair. Says it's full of secrets."

"He can teleport anywhere. Even if we flush him out, we need to find a way to capture him. He has to be separated from the stone." He slid down over the rocks. "I'll take a look."

"Be wary. Chopper will have his lair protected."

Grey Cloak signaled to Zanna and Zora. They moved toward Tiny's position as he approached the burrow on cat's paws. Grey Cloak squatted down and looked inside. Tiny had been right. The wormhole underneath the rocks was barely big enough for a gnome to squeeze through, let alone an elf.

"I can do this. I have to." On knees and elbows, Grey Cloak crawled underneath the rock's shadow. He lowered to a belly crawl and squeezed into the hole.

To his surprise, he made his way through the tight tunnel with relative ease. The Cloak of Legends had something to do with it, he was sure. Inside the cloak, he was always able to move without restrictions. He was never too hot or too cold, no matter the climate, and he could swim like a fish and breath underwater.

The biggest problem was the darkness. The tunnel was pitch black.

He crawled a few body lengths deep then stopped. Turning an ear, he listened for any signs of life. *Nothing.*

He resumed the agonizing crawl. Gnomes were known for their toiling underneath the surface. Large groups would build an expansive network of tunnels and underground villages. He'd heard they could spread out for miles, even leagues. He hoped that wasn't the case then.

With his knees and elbows propelling him through the dirt, he made it several dozen yards deeper then stopped again. The sound of trickling water pricked his ears. There was something else too.

Is that singing? Humming? He picked up the pace.

The tunnel opened into a small underground cavern. Like a campfire, a pile of rocks glowed in the cavern's center, giving off a soft illumination. Baubles and trinkets of all sorts of things surrounded the pile, large and small. Brass candlesticks, finely crafted hairpins and combs, delicate jewelry boxes brimming with necklaces, bracelets, and earrings. There was a collection of pipes on a small shelf, knives, daggers, and a nest of jewels in a golden bowl a man could eat out of.

There was more, much more, but Grey Cloak had seen enough. He didn't hear anything. *Wait, where's the singing?*

The small area had quieted. There wasn't so much as a scratch or a scuffle.

He must have heard me. Zooks.

It wouldn't take anything for Chopper to vanish in a wink of a lash. If spooked, he would scurry off. There weren't any other exits to note in the area. The walls were dirt and rock from top to bottom.

The Cloak of Legends sent a pulse of warm energy into Grey Cloak's body. He looked up as hundreds of legs skittered across the ceiling toward him. The giant centipedes were as long as a man's arm and had white bodies and bright pink eyes.

Nasty creatures.

He noticed needlelike spines on their backs then a long sharp barb on the tips of their tails. They split up and scurried toward him from three different directions.

I knew I should have brought the Rod of Weapons. But the squeeze was too tight.

He snaked a dagger out of his belt and stayed buried in his hole. There was only one direction they could attack him from. *Come at me, bugs, and taste my dagger.* He reasoned that it shouldn't take much to kill one of those things with a little dose of wizard fire.

The Cloak of Legends pulsed again. That time, the sensation came from down around his legs. He twisted his head around. "Oh no."

An albino centipede hurdled through the tunnel behind him, charging his feet.

"Jumping jugglers!" Grey Cloak squirted out of the tunnel and dropped down to the main cavern.

Four ugly centipedes became eight as more of them wriggled out of the pores of the wall. The swarm kept coming, growing in number until they covered the floor and ceiling.

His skin crawled. He wanted to jump out of it. "There are too many!" He charged the dagger with wizard fire.

The oversized bugs stopped and hunched their spines upward. They surrounded Grey Cloak and fired their quills from all directions.

He wrapped himself in the cloak. Hundreds of quills bounced off of the fabric.

That was close.

Cloak or no cloak, the multitude of monsters resumed their ground attack. They scurried across the floor and dropped from the ceiling.

"Zooks!" Grey Cloak covered himself up in the Cloak of Legends. He sank to the floor, making himself as small as possible, blanketing every inch of his body.

The centipedes piled on layer by layer.

He collapsed under their weight with the sickening, suffocating feeling of their nasty legs crawling all over him. "This is disgusting! Gaaah!"

13

The albino centipedes covered him from head to toe, trying to worm their bodies through the Cloak of Legends.

Grey Cloak gritted his teeth. *I've had enough of this!*

He summoned the wizard fire and let it build. Unleashing his energy, he fed a strong pulse of it through his cloak. *Die, you vile things, die!*

The Cloak of Legends filled with blue radiance, then the wizard fire exploded. *Poomph!*

The shock wave of energy sent the giant insects flying in all directions. Their crusty exoskeletons turned crisp, and they balled up into pinwheels.

Grey Cloak peeked through his cloak. The survivors had scurried back into the burrows in the walls. Dozens of the others lay dead at his feet.

"Yuck. Nasty little things stink as bad as they look once you cook them." He shook the carcasses of the dried-up bugs from his cloak. He picked a curled one up. The ball was a little bigger than his hand. *Well, Tiny said there'd be traps.* He chucked it and kicked several others away.

When Chopper showed up next, he would probably be spooked and vanish again. Grey Cloak rubbed his chest through the fabric of his cloak. "We'll have to be ready."

The longer he wore it, the bigger a part of him the Cloak of Legends became. It was like a second skin and old friend. He'd caught himself talking to it before. No doubt the cloak had protected him, but the connection between the two had become stronger.

He squatted down in front of the glowing rocks and sawed his finger under his lip. "Chopper isn't a bad gnome. We're friends, after all. Perhaps I can appeal to his softer side." Unsure whether he was speaking to himself or the cloak, he added, "Maybe we can trick him. Playing dead might work."

To his chagrin, Grey picked up a few centipedes and started to unroll them. He lay flat on his back by the pile of glow rocks then covered himself in the creatures. He shifted his arms and legs in a disheveled position, contorting them somewhat as if he was wounded.

"Now, we wait," he whispered. "No doubt he'll come back to see who invaded his abode. I would." He closed his eyes.

The heat from the glowing rocks kept his face warm. The minerals were unique, and he'd seen them before in the undead city of Thannis, where they illuminated the caverns like stars. The radiance was soothing. Perhaps too soothing.

Grey Cloak's eyes were already closed, but they also became heavy. He'd forgotten the last time he rested, as he didn't often sleep much at all. He'd been drawing on his wizard fire, and the drain had finally caught up with him.

He yawned. "That's not a good thing. Cloak, don't let me sleep."

Another yawn came.

The comforting folds of the cloak swaddled him like a warm baby's blanket.

Grey Cloak drifted off to sleep.

A PULSE of energy woke him up. How long he slept, he had no idea, but alertness filled him. He kept his eyes closed.

The scuffle of bare feet caught his ears. Someone sobbed.

"No," Chopper's scratchy, soft voice said. He set something down, and a chicken clucked. "My friend, Grey Cloak. My centipedes have killed him."

Footsteps came closer. He felt Chopper's breath on his face. The gnome shook his shoulder. "Don't be dead, friend. Don't be dead, I couldn't bear it."

The dead centipedes slid off of Grey Cloak's body. He felt it through the cloak as if it was his own skin.

"Eh? What is this? My pets are dead? What sort of trickery is this?"

Grey Cloak formed a picture of where Chopper stood in his

mind. He struck out in an instant, seizing the sand gnome by the ankle and the wrist. "Chopper, give me back the stone!"

The startled white hen clucked and half flew across the cave.

The stone appeared in his free hand, and Chopper got a crazed look in his eyes. "Never! Let go of me! It's mine!"

In the next moment, they were both transported through space and time. They reappeared in the sky, high above the clouds.

"Let go!" Chopper fought off Grey Cloak as they plunged through the air. "You can't do this!"

"But I can!" Grey Cloak said. He'd used the stone before and knew whatever he touched came with him. "I'm holding on no matter what. We need the stone to save the world!"

Chopper's fuzzy, impish face became demonic. "Bug snot on the world! I don't care! This is my stone!"

They vanished then reappeared in snowy mountain tops.

"You want to play games?" Chopper asked, straining to wiggle his wrist and ankle free. "I'll freeze you to death in the heights."

As far as Grey Cloak could tell, they were in the mountains of Ice Vale. The bitter cold in the peaks could freeze a person to death, but Grey Cloak had the cloak.

"Nice try, but that isn't going to work!" He squeezed. "You're our friend—you can't betray us. We need the stone!"

Chopper screamed in his face. "Never!"

In the next moment, Grey Cloak found himself underneath the surface of a body of water. Colorful fish scattered in all directions.

The little furball will try anything. I have to end this now.

His cloak's power gave him the same free movement below water as he had above. He released Chopper's ankle and seized the gnome's other wrist that had the stone in hand.

Chopper planted his feet in Grey Cloak's chest and fought to kick out. The wiry gnome was strong, perhaps stronger than him with the stone enhancing his power.

Grey Cloak's grip started to weaken and slip. He caught Chopper's triumphant underwater grin.

Enough of this! He bit down on Chopper's hand with all of his might. Using the knuckles in his free hand, he punched the gnome square in the solar plexus.

Bubbles erupted out of Chopper's mouth. The green stone fell from his grasp and sank toward the bottom.

Grey Cloak swam after the Stone of Transport and snatched it in his hand before it hit bottom. He turned and saw the gnome drifting toward the floor. He wasn't moving.

Zooks. I must have hit him too hard.

He swam up and grabbed Chopper. Using the stone's power, he teleported them both out of the water. They reappeared in the rocky plains where he'd left Tiny. He stood—gnome in hand—among the gaping faces of the cyclops, Zanna, Gorva, Zora, and Streak.

"Why are you all wet?" Zora asked.

"Don't ask." Grey Cloak squeezed the water out of Chopper and shook him.

The soggy little gnome came to. "Eh, what happened?" He stiffened. "Where's my stone?"

Grey Cloak had hidden it in his inner pocket. "It's not *your* stone."

"Give it back! Give it back!"

Tiny swallowed up Chopper in his hands and picked him up off the ground. "You've been bad. Do you know what trouble you caused?"

"No!" But his defiant tone changed, and he made a sorrowful face. "Yes. I'm sorry. Now can I have it back?"

Tiny ignored Chopper's request and nodded once toward Dwarf Skull. "You guys better go. I'll take Chopper home—far away from all of you."

"Thanks, Tiny." Grey Cloak squeezed the water out of his hair. "Saddle up, everyone. It's time to go."

14

TIME MURAL CHAMBER

The elven sorceress Tatiana stood in front of the Time Portal archway and looked directly at the foreboding and humongous figure of Black Frost.

Magnolia, Dirklen's sister and a former Risker, stood beside her, twisting a bouncy strand of blond hair around her finger. The women were about the same height but were both formidable and beautiful in their own ways.

Dalsay, a living apparition dressed in full wizard robes, monitored the shiny gemstones in the Pedestal of Power. Meanwhile, Nath, an oversized, long-haired hermit of a man from another world, sat on one of two pewter thrones, his strong, grizzled chin resting in the palm of his hand.

Nath yawned. "That's one big dragon. And trust me, I've seen a lot of big dragons."

Tatiana and Magnolia turned and gave him an irritated look.

"Any advice to offer?" Tatiana asked.

He shrugged. "The bigger they are, the harder they fall."

She shook her head and sighed. Black Frost's height rivaled the towers. The scale plates on the humongous creature's body were bigger than most men. He was a mountain—a moving fortress—and was about to destroy one of the last towers.

"What is he waiting for?" Magnolia crossed her arms, cradling her elbows. Her eyes were fixed on the tiny figure of a man standing on Black Frost's shoulder. "He's been staring the tower down for half a day. What do you suppose Dirklen—I mean, Gossamer—is saying to him?"

"He's buying more time. He has to be. Apparently, Gossamer has been very convincing leading Black Frost back to the north," Tatiana said.

She'd helped devise a plan to disguise Gossamer as Dirklen and create a diversion. Gossamer had planted the idea that the heroes in the tower were planning to draw the dragon south while they attempted an insurrection of Black Frost's temple in the north. Currently, even though all of the towers were connected, her group remained in the tower farthest in the southeast, near the Great River.

Black Frost had begun an invasion of all the towers. Destroying them would destroy the Time Mural, the largest threat to defeat him. He'd succeeded in destroying almost every one, and as each tower fell, another weakened.

The heroes fought tooth and nail to buy time, salvage the Helm of the Dragons, and build the all-destructive artifact from another world. That time was running out. In a matter of days,

Black Frost could wipe out all of the remaining towers, and it would be over.

"I don't know about you, but my skin is crawling underneath my armor," Magnolia said as she watched Gossamer and Black Frost converse. "My gut tells me that Black Frost isn't buying Gossamer's story. He hesitates. Black Frost doesn't hesitate."

"We have to have faith in Gossamer. If Black Frost didn't trust him, why would he go back to Dark Mountain?" Tatiana asked.

Magnolia traced the ugly scar that ran down along her cheek. "Good question. I don't know."

Gossamer, disguised as Dirklen, paced back and forth on a small patch of Black Frost's shoulder. *What is he thinking?*

He believed he'd persuaded Black Frost to destroy the northernmost tower, yet the dragon overlord abstained. On the one hand, Black Frost's hesitation gave them more time. On the other, it meant something was amiss.

"Dirklen," Black Frost said. "Come closer."

Gossamer levitated before the dragon's face. "Yes, Wonderous One?"

"I'd have expected you to have received word from your sister. If she is loyal to us, why hasn't she opened the Wizard Watch?"

"As much as I hate to think it, it is possible that she perished. Or she has been captured."

Black Frost snorted. "Use the stones you've acquired and find out."

Gossamer's throat tightened. He pulled the satchel around from his side to his chest. "As you wish. I'll need to discern how to use their powers. I'm not sure which stone is which, but it won't take long for me to master them."

Black Frost's voice turned threatening. "Don't delay. I want you to go in there and destroy our remaining enemies. Perhaps you will save your sister at the same time, and we can maintain control of their Time Mural."

Gossamer felt for certain Black Frost would take down the tower. Instead, he wanted to regain control of it. *Gooseberries!*

He would have to gamble with his life and defy Black Frost. "The mere existence of the Time Mural will always pose a threat. As much as I adore my sister, it would be best for her to perish along with the rest of the towers."

Black Frost raised a brow. "You question me?"

"I fear you might play into their hands. They are crafty." He bowed. "If I may be so bold, I'd destroy them all. I'd destroy them all now and move on to the next world, your majesty."

The great dragon gave Gossamer a sniff. "I can smell your fear. Do I smell deceit as well?"

He's onto me. Gossamer raised his head and replied, "The only thing you should smell is victory."

Black Frost narrowed his eyes. "Victory is certain, but you I'm not so certain about."

15

Inside the Wizard Watch, Magnolia buckled on her sword belt. "I need to get out there. Take me to the top of the tower. I need to see Black Frost."

Tatiana shook her head. "You'll spoil all that Gossamer has worked for. You need to let him—"

"No! I trust my gut on this. Black Frost is delaying. He's sniffing us out. Otherwise, he'd have been more decisive."

Tatiana gave Dalsay an uncertain look. "What do you think?"

"I fear she may be right. Black Frost is known for swift action," the ghostly mage said. "I'll take her to the top with your agreement."

Tatiana laid a hand on Magnolia's shoulder. "Go. We'll be watching."

Dalsay drifted out from behind the Pedestal of Power then led Magnolia out of the Time Mural chamber.

Tatiana was left alone with Nath. "For someone who needs to have his world saved, you're very silent."

Nath sat up on the throne. "If I'd do anything different than what you are doing, I'd speak up." He locked his scaly fingers and cracked his knuckles. He pressed one of the gemstone buttons on the broad arm of his throne. "I'll be ready to use the tower's cannons on a moment's notice. I have a knack for using these chairs."

"I don't think the tower's weapons will do any good against Black Frost." She moved behind the pedestal.

"No, but they wreak havoc on his forces." Nath's fingers moved over the stones. The image in the Time Mural shifted. Thousands of Black Guard troops surrounded the tower. All of them were foot soldiers, led by Riskers on land and in the skies.

"We need to save energy. Our efforts will be as useless against those numbers. There are too many of them."

Nath shook his head. "I learned long ago that evil never rests. It won't hesitate to take you down. You can't hesitate to take them down either."

Tatiana nodded. She passed her hand over the top of the stones, and the image in the archway shifted again. Magnolia stood alone on the flat top of the tower. The high winds tore at her hair. She brushed the strands away with her fingers. Arms high, she flagged Black Frost down. At once, Riskers swooped over top of her, their arrows poised to fire.

Tatiana's chest tightened. "I hope she knows what she's doing."

"Yes, we're about to find out." Nath leaned forward.

Black Frost marched toward the tower and reached out with his paw.

"Well, it appears that your sister has decided to join you, Dirklen," Black Frost stated. "It will be a family reunion. What a nice surprise."

Gossamer turned midair. Magnolia stood on the top of the tower, frantically waving her arms.

No, what is she doing? His thoughts raced. *She must think as I think. He's onto us. She wants us to convince him otherwise.*

Black Frost approached Magnolia, stretched out his arm, and laid it on the tower, making a bridge. He opened up his palm for her.

Magnolia's heart thumped in her chest. *Lords of the air, he's humongous!*

With effort, she climbed onto Black Frost's massive paw and stood.

He brought his hand toward his face and said, "Join your sister, Dirklen."

Gossamer landed by Magnolia. They stood shoulder to shoulder.

"Brother and sister, together again." Black Frost's breath

steamed up their hair as he spoke. "What is our situation, Magnolia? Have you conquered the enemy in my towers?"

She bowed. "There are only two survivors, but they have exiled me. But we have the stones. Together, we can invade and conquer them once and for all." She looked him dead in the eye. "They are weak. Desperate. Now is the time to deliver the final crushing blow."

"Interesting. Dirklen and I were discussing a similar strategy," the dragon overlord said.

The muscles between Magnolia's shoulder blades bunched up. Black Frost kept his plans close to his scales. *He'd never ask Dirklen or me for advice. Either he's getting overconfident or—*

"Now that I have you both together, my concerns are confirmed." He sniffed them both. "Your blood is not the same. One of you is an imposter." He looked at Gossamer. "And that would be you, wouldn't it, elf?"

Without any control from him, Gossamer's transformation into Dirklen was undone. He faced Black Frost. "It appears I am found out."

Magnolia made a shocked look and gasped. "I had no idea of this deception! I swear it!"

"It's true," Gossamer stated. "Magnolia had no knowledge of my disguise."

"Don't take me for a fool, elf. I don't believe any words from either of your lips." Black Frost eyed the satchel. "I take it that those are not the stones that I seek. Clever. Your deception worked for a time, but it won't make a difference. Nothing can stop me, especially not puny creatures like you!"

"No matter, Black Frost!" Gossamer said in his loudest voice. "If you were so powerful, you'd have destroyed all of the towers by now. So long as one stands, you cannot win! You won't! You have lost!"

Black Frost's talons closed around the both of them.

Magnolia drew her sword. "Gossamer, go!" She stabbed the dragon's palm. It was no more than a needle in a giant's hand. Black Frost's claws closed around them both.

Magnolia shouted her last word. "Hurry!"

16

Nath fired the tower's mystic cannons at Black Frost.

Tatiana's heart stopped in her chest. Right before her eyes, Magnolia and Gossamer were crushed in Black Frost's grip.

"No," she muttered. "No!"

Torpedoes of energy struck the dragon overlord in the neck, but his grip didn't loosen. The jarring impact of the missiles didn't sway him either.

"You're right. These cannons don't faze him at all." Nath adjusted the picture in the archway and aimed at a Risker on a grand dragon soaring through the sky. "Time to switch to a smaller target." He pressed the buttons on the arm of the chair.

A bright green torpedo shot out of the tower and blasted the Risker out of the air.

"Woo-hooo! That's more like it." Nath aimed the mural's image at the troops on the ground. "Look at them, standing around doing nothing. Time to send them a message. This is war!"

A series of torpedoes sent the Black Guard flying in all directions. Bodies were blown apart. Weapons and armor went flying, wounding more soldiers with their own gear.

Gossamer reappeared in front of the Time Mural. He was huddled over, shaking like a leaf. "I tried to save her. I tried."

Tatiana rushed to his side, sat him up, and held him tight. "It's not your fault. The teleport ring only carries one. You're blessed to be alive."

Gossamer took the satchel off of his shoulder and set it on the floor. He poured out the fake Thunderstones and the Star of Light.

"Magnolia saved me." He gave Tatiana a sad look. "Black Frost knew, but I don't think he did for sure until she arrived. Why did you let her leave? I could have teleported out of harm's way."

"She sensed the danger and insisted. Magnolia wanted to do what she thought was right. Perhaps dupe Black Frost and buy more time," she said. "It's not your fault, Gossamer."

The disheveled black-and-white robes rustled as the elven sorcerer fought his way back to his feet. Tatiana steadied him as they looked into the Time Mural.

Rows of Black Guard soldiers were being wiped out by the mystic cannons.

Nath's golden eyes were molten fire. "Sometimes it's fun to go after the low-hanging fruit."

"Enough, Nath! We need to save our energy! Desist!" Tatiana called.

"One more." He took aim at another enemy dragon rider flying in the opposite direction. "Release the hounds!"

A torpedo hit man and dragon square in the back. The rider flew out of the saddle, and the dragon reared up, wings spread wide. It dropped out of the sky and crushed a dozen troops.

Nath raised his hands from the chair. He said in his scratchy voice, "I guess the fun is over."

"For us, it is," Dalsay said. "I'm taking control of the Time Mural."

Black Frost took over the entire archway. He held Magnolia's crushed body in the palm of his taloned grip then cast her aside into the mass of soldiers below his feet.

"Poor woman," Nath said.

"What do you think Black Frost is going to do?" Tatiana asked Gossamer.

Gossamer shuffled toward the archway. "I goaded him into destroying the tower as planned. He considered saving it and taking over the Time Mural, but I gave him more food for thought, telling him as long as it existed, we'd always have a way to kill him."

Nath leaned forward in his throne. "It looks like your words worked." He pointed at the image.

The seams in between the scales of Black Frost's chest turned fiery bright. They lit up in his lower belly and worked their way up.

Tatiana hurried over to the chamber door and pushed the

floor lever, closing it. "Dalsay, keep the shields up until we are completely cut off from the northern tower. We can't make it simple for Black Frost."

Black Frost opened his mouth, and azure dragon fire came out. The entire image in the mural was a waterfall of roaring flame.

Gossamer shielded his face and backed away from the archway. He stumbled on the dais. "The heat is tremendous."

The stone walls warmed up, and the cracks between them glowed blue. The walls quaked.

"I can't hold the shield any longer. It will drain all of the energy we have left," Dalsay warned.

She nodded. "Cut it off. All of it."

Dalsay manipulated his hands over the stones. The mural in the archway quivered then went black. She watched the walls cool. The connection to the tower near Dark Mountain had been severed, with everyone safe in the southern tower.

"There are only three towers left. This one, Crow Valley, and the Wilds of Arrowwood," Tatiana said as she gazed at the blank wall in the archway. "We can move to any tower we wish, but once they all fall, hope falls with them."

BLACK FROST'S breath sent his soldiers retreating from their positions near the tower's base. Hundreds were consumed by the flames. His wroth fire burst through the seams inside the tower's stones. It burned from the inside out like a chimney fire through a smokestack.

Dousing his stream of omnipotent flame, he watched the Wizard Watch burn from top to bottom. As a plume of black smoke rose from the great pillar, the troops on the ground cheered.

In a final motion, Black Frost pushed the brittle tower over. The Black Guard members caught in the resulting inferno screamed. Scores of men were crushed underneath tons of fiery rock.

Finally, the dragon overlord summoned his Riskers. A ring of dragon riders flew around his head.

"We fly south. The tower in Arrowwood is next." Black Frost spread his wings. "There will be no rest. I'll lead the way."

17

DWARF SKULL

Hands behind his back, Grey Cloak paced the road in front of the dwarven armory's entrance. He and the others—Razor, Gorva, Zora, and Shannon—waited outside, but the minutes seemed like hours, the hours like days.

Razor sat with his back against the wall, tossing a dagger in the air. "I feel like I'm waiting for one of my sisters to give birth. How long is this baby going to take?"

Gorva snatched his dagger out of the air. "You're going to cut yourself."

"Ah, you care." Razor snaked out another dagger from his belt and began juggling it, end over end. "I have to admit, the balance from this Sky Rider steel is perfect. I wish I'd had access to this metal years ago."

Zora stopped biting her nails and made her way over to the pacing Grey Cloak. "You're going to wear a hole in the road."

"And you're going to nibble your fingernails off." He eyed the huge barn doors that accessed the armory. "I think I'll take a peek."

The elven rogue hooked his arm. "I don't think that's wise. Remember what Rhonna said? Anyone that interrupts will have a limb taken off."

"Well, we can't wait here all day. They need to finish, and they need to finish quickly."

Dyphestive, Crane, and Zanna came down the street. Dyphestive chewed on a leg of meat the size of his head. Crane carried a jug in one hand and a basket in the other. Only Zanna was empty-handed.

"We brought sustenance," Crane said with his friendly smile. "Dwarven bread and cheeses, plus a jug of their finest ale." He hiccupped. "Enjoy. It will last you for a day or days even."

Grey Cloak frowned. "We don't have days. Dyphestive, knock on the door. Rhonna likes you better."

Dyphestive shoved a hunk of meat into his mouth and shook his head. "Uh-uh. I know better than that. If they want to be left alone, we'd better listen."

"Perhaps time is not as pressing as you fear," Zanna suggested. "Use the Stone of Transport and check in with Tatiana."

"I can't access the towers unless they know I'm coming. Their defenses will be up."

"Why don't some of us return to Safe Haven while the rest wait?" Zora asked. "Use the stone to take us there instead."

"That's the best idea I've heard all day." Grey Cloak hooked his arm around Zora's waist and said, "Hang on."

"No, waaaiiit—"

But it was too late for her to object. They reappeared inside Safe Haven's vault, beside the Eye of the Sky Rider's pedestal.

Grey Cloak steadied Zora from behind. "How do you feel?"

"Like I've been transported between time and space." She started to wiggle free of his grasp.

He spun her into his arms and looked down into her eyes. With his hands resting in the small of her back, he said, "It's been a long time since we've been alone. An entire dragon's lair all to ourselves."

Zora leaned back and started to push away. "What are you getting at?"

He pulled her up on her toes and kissed her.

Zora pushed away at first, but then her lips softened. Her hands slid up his back and into his hair.

They kissed passionately for what felt like a long time. She melted into his arms as they sank to the floor. Then they broke it off, panting.

She lay on his chest. "Perhaps that was long overdue."

"Seeing how the world might end, I'd want my last moment to be like this—with you." He bent over and kissed her softly again. "I think you're beautiful, Zora."

"Yes, well. I've always been fond of you, too, you know. Since the first time we met."

"Oh, since the day you stole from me?"

She nuzzled his chest. "It turned out for the better, didn't it?"

He arched his eyebrows and gave a small shrug.

"I saw that," she said. "It's not over, Grey Cloak. You'll think of something." She crawled over him and gave him a long kiss.

"Ahem."

When their lips parted, they found themselves looking up at Dalsay.

"Sorry to interrupt, but now is no time to start a family," the wizened sorcerer said.

Grey Cloak and Zora helped each other to their feet, but their hands remained clasped.

"What's going on, Dalsay?" Grey Cloak asked.

"Black Frost has destroyed the tower east of Dark Mountain. Magnolia is dead."

Zora gasped.

"Dead?" Grey Cloak gave him an incredulous look. "What happened?"

"She tried to deceive Black Frost and save Gossamer." Dalsay stroked his beard into a point. "She did save Gossamer at least. The plan worked, but we fear Black Frost is going to take down the last three towers even quicker." He moved to the Eye of the Sky Rider. "I came to chart his course. If you'll excuse me."

"This is awful news." Zora teared up. "I know Magnolia was an enemy for the longest time, but I'd begun to like her."

"Her past might have caught up with her, but in my heart," the elder wizard said, "I feel she redeemed herself."

"She committed a brave act. Sacrificed herself for a cause." Dalsay's hands waved over the pedestal's eye. "I take it your mission was a success."

"Rhonna and the dwarves are building the Apparatus of Ruune as we speak, but I don't know how long it will take. She won't tell me." Grey Cloak peered into the image in the bowl. "Where is he?"

"Hold on." Dalsay spread the image out with his fingers, revealing the beautiful landscape of Gapoli. "Everything appears so tranquil from this point of view. Yet on the surface is a world in turmoil."

"There!" Grey Cloak pointed at a black dot moving across the skies.

Dalsay pinched his fingers together and zoomed in on the massive dragon, Black Frost. "He's on a path to the tower in the Wilds. Judging by his speed, he'll be there in less than a day." He nodded at them. "I must warn Tatiana."

"What about us?"

Dalsay started to fade away, but before he did, the stoic mage said, "Go back and tell Queen Rhonna that she'd better hurry or we'll all be dead soon enough."

18

When Grey Cloak returned to Dwarf Skull, he was alone. A squad of twelve dwarven soldiers stood at the entrance to the armory. Battle-axes in hand, they were in full armor and didn't bat an eye at his arrival.

"What's this? Why the soldiers?" he asked his friends still waiting near the entrance.

Everyone in Talon's group averted their eyes, except for Zanna, who came forward. "It's my fault. I snuck in and took a peek."

"And?"

A bit shamefaced, she said, "I was caught before I even got a glimpse. I can't believe the stubby-fingered bearded ones caught me." She shook her head. "Me of all people. They made it look as if Crane wandered in there."

Crane's mouth opened into an O.

"Don't say a word," Zanna warned him. "But it is my fault. Now the armory is sealed up tighter than a drum. What's the word from the Wizard Watch?"

"Bad."

The six of them gathered around Grey Cloak.

"How bad?" Dyphestive asked.

"Gossamer's disguise worked. It bought us time, but the Wizard Watch near Dark Mountain is destroyed. And," he said with a sad face, "Magnolia perished."

"Perished?" Dyphestive asked. "How?"

"She tried to help Gossamer with his deception. Black Frost saw through them. He escaped, but she didn't."

Razor's palms shifted on his sword pommels. "Sounds like her wicked past did her in. It happens."

Everyone gave him a disappointed look.

"What? It's true. Magnolia took out a lot of good people. In the end, she paid the price." Razor looked at Gorva. "Am I wrong?"

"No," Gorva said. "You are right."

"I don't disagree." Grey Cloak frowned sadly. "But Magnolia tried to right her wrongs. She gave her life for us."

A moment of silence passed.

Zanna broke it. "What now?"

"Black Frost is on his way to the Wizard Watch in the Wilds of Arrowwood. He'll have it destroyed in a day." Grey Cloak moved over to the wall and picked up the Rod of Weapons. "There is no slowing him. I'd imagine he'll destroy the Wizard

Watch in the southeast next, and then he'll arrive here. And he won't be alone either. He still has scores of Riskers in his command, not to mention ground troops. They are marching this way from the north as we speak." He looked at the armory's doors. "If we don't have that weapon built by then, well... we will all be doomed."

"Once all of the towers are lost, there won't be any way to stop him," Zanna said. "The entire world will be devastated. But we still have the Helm of the Dragons. It's possible that it might work against him."

"Only if someone is strong enough to use it. It practically killed Zora and Tatiana. And we need Tatiana to control the Time Mural and protect the towers." Grey Cloak spun his rod behind his back then flipped it out again. "One of us will have to be ready to use it as a last defense."

"So, we wait?" Shannon asked.

Grey Cloak shrugged. "And hope. That's all that we can do at the moment. Everyone, rest. You'll need your strength one way or the other. Get some food. Eat, drink, enjoy."

"You don't have to make it sound like it's our last meal." Razor nudged Gorva. "Come, let's go to the mead hall. I could use something to eat and drink."

"I'll go," Crane said.

Shannon followed after the three as well.

"So," Dyphestive said, "Zora didn't come back."

"She wanted to help Tatiana. I took her from Safe Haven to the tower." Grey Cloak watched the others move on out of earshot and disappear around the next block. "I was thinking—"

"Oh no," Zanna said.

"Hear me out. We might be able to stop Black Frost before he gets this far. Or slow him down."

"What did you have in mind?" Dyphestive asked.

"One of us should try using the Helm of the Dragons. After all, we are naturals. If one of us is strong enough, we might be able to control him."

Dyphestive shook his head. "Sounds dangerous. We don't know the risks."

"No, but we need to find out. I can use the Stone of Transport and teleport to his location using the Eye of the Sky Rider. I can at least test it out. After all, nothing ventured, nothing gained."

"You'll need to keep one of us with you. And I'd talk with Zora and Tatiana too. They will be able to share with you what to expect," Zanna suggested. "But I'm not so sure that you are the one that should be doing this."

"Why?"

"You're our leader. We can't have anything happen to you."

"If I'm the leader, it's all the more reason why I should take the risk."

Dyphestive laid a hand on his brother's shoulder. "No, I think she is right, brother. You can't put yourself in further danger. It is your efforts that keep hope alive. We need your mind to be sound. We can't afford it to be scrambled." He glanced at both of them. "Perhaps *I* should try. After all, I can heal from any damage that might be done."

Grey Cloak grabbed ahold of Zanna and Dyphestive. "Let's

pay our friends a visit at the Wizard Watch, and we'll see what they think."

They both nodded.

Zanna said, "Lead the way. Or take us away, rather."

He summoned the stone's power, and the three of them vanished right before the dwarven soldier's unblinking eyes.

19

"Are you out of your skull?" Zora said to Grey Cloak. They'd reunited in the Time Mural chamber, along with Dyphestive, Gossamer, Dalsay, Zanna, Tatiana, and Nath. "We can't risk losing you to the artifact. Believe me, my gray matter still rattles."

"I'll take my chances."

Arms crossed, Zora rolled her eyes. "Oh, here we go again."

Grey Cloak peered over her shoulder as Dyphestive took the dais steps to the thrones in one giant stride. The Helm of the Dragons was on the throne to the left of Nath. He picked it up.

Underneath the stones, the helmet's metal shone like molten silver. All of the dragon charms were embedded in the metal, each a different color, shape, and size, in an almost mosaic pattern.

Dyphestive tilted the helmet side to side. "Seems small." He lifted it up.

Tatiana tilted her head. "What is he doing?"

"He wanted to give it a try," Grey Cloak replied.

Dyphestive tried to stuff his head into the helmet.

"I've already tried it," Tatiana reminded him. "It drained me."

"You take on all of the dragon minds at once. You can feel their thoughts and feelings," Zora added.

"We aren't worried about all of the dragons. We are only worried about Black Frost." Grey Cloak moved up on the platform and tried to help Dyphestive into the helmet. He climbed on the throne and stood over him, trying to push the helmet down. Straining, he said, "We only need to get a simple command through to Black Frost, such as sleep, turn back, or stop. Something that will slow him down. This is what you built the helm for, isn't it?"

"To control dragons, yes, but it has limitations as well as risks. Black Frost's mind is a wall of iron," Tatiana said as she pulled up different images of the tower in the Wilds up in the Time Mural. "He's prepared for such an attack."

Grey Cloak gave up and pulled the helmet off Dyphestive. It didn't even make it down to the tops of his ears. "They definitely had a smaller person in mind when they created this. I thought it would shrink and grow to fit the wearer. Hmm, let me try."

"No!" Zora rushed up the platform.

"What? There aren't any dragons around. I can get used to it." He eyed the artifact. "Though a helmet isn't my style. Way too bulky."

He slipped it on. The snug helmet fit his head like a glove and felt unusually light. "It's not so bad, and I don't think I'm going mad." He smiled. "I feel enlightened."

Tatiana and Zora exchanged uncertain looks.

"Tatiana, can you use the Time Mural to look farther out? I'm certain that Black Frost will send many scouts ahead. If we spot them, I can test out the helmet's power."

"I can try," answered Tatiana.

Gossamer joined her behind the Pedestal of Power. "I'd be happy to assist."

The image in the archway began in the beautiful forests of Arrowwood. It rose above the treetops and sailed north.

"Thanks to the Eye of the Sky Rider, we've been able to exercise similar abilities with the Time Mural." Tatiana's eyebrows knitted together. "It will still be like finding a needle in a haystack with all of this open sky."

Grey Cloak closed his eyes. "I wonder whether I can sense them?"

Dalsay floated to the thrones. "The dragon charms are designed to control dragons, but it is possible it could be used to locate them too. It would be a matter of pulling them out of hiding. They are drawn to the enchanted stone. It captivates them. Bear in mind, we are not close to what we are seeing. In the tower's immediate vicinity is one thing. Leagues, or rather scores of leagues, are another."

Grey Cloak's fingers tickled the air at his side. He pictured dragons. *Hmm... I wonder whether I can contact Streak.*

He envisioned his dragon and tried to call out to him. *Streak. Can you hear me?*

His efforts were met with silence. At the moment, he didn't feel the wave of energy spreading through his body as Zora had described. The thoughts of a dozen dragons didn't merge with his mind either. He was alone, in his own shell, searching for enemy dragons.

"Boss?"

Grey Cloak heard Streak's voice in his mind. He tried replying. *Streak! You can hear me?*

"I hear you, but I don't see you. I thought you returned to the Wizard Watch," Streak answered telepathically. "How are you doing that?"

I'm using the Helm of the Dragons. I'm in the tower, far away. Ha! This is fantastic!

"What's going on?" Tatiana asked.

Grey Cloak opened his eyes. "I'm talking to Streak. Mind to mind. It's fantastic."

"You have a strong connection with him already," Dalsay stated. "Perhaps that is why it works. Try to reach another dragon you know well. Cinder perhaps."

"I don't know if Anya will like that, but I'll try," Grey Cloak said. *Streak, is Cinder near?*

"I haven't seen him since the battle," Streak replied. "Why?"

I wanted to try to reach out to him. Hold on.

He focused on a clear picture of Cinder in his mind. *Cinder, can you hear me?*

"It's still me, boss. You're talking in my head," Streak replied.

Everyone's attention had been taken up by Grey Cloak, but Zora's eyes were locked on the mural. "Pardon the interruption, but I see a dragon."

Tatiana tore her gaze away from Grey Cloak and looked into the archway. "Where, sister?"

Zora pointed to the upper left-hand corner. "There."

"I see. Let me adjust the image." Tatiana's hands gyrated over the warm, scintillating glow of the stones. "Hmm, it appears they have a grand dragon leading the scouts. I'd expected a knot of middlings..." Her voice trailed off as the image zoomed in closer.

Zora stepped back. "That's not a grand. Oh my. Tell me that's not what I think it is!"

Grey Cloak turned to stare at the Time Mural. A humongous dragon surrounded by smaller ones that looked like birds on an ox's back flew right at them. His blood froze. "Jumping jugglers, that's Black Frost, isn't it?"

The mural zoomed in. There was no mistaking the great dragon's blazing blue eyes.

"It is," Tatiana replied.

"How far away is he?" Grey Cloak asked.

"Twenty leagues," the sorceress said. She swung her gaze toward him. "He'll be here within the hour."

Grey Cloak looked at his brother. "Zooks."

20

In a hushed voice, Tatiana stared at the Time Mural and said, "How did he get here so fast?"

"Black Frost's powers are boundless. If I were to venture to guess, he's enhanced the abilities of his Riskers as well," Dalsay said. "Perhaps because he is so large, we underestimated his speed."

Zora looked at Grey Cloak. "What are we going to do?"

He adjusted the Helm of the Dragons on his head. "We'll do what we have to."

Nath rose from his seat, stood between the brothers, and put his hands on their shoulders. "It looks like you have your work cut out for you." Then he whispered in Grey Cloak's ear, "Remember, dragons are intelligent beasts. Work with them. Don't push. Bend."

Grey Cloak's hands, normally dry as a bone, turned clammy.

He rubbed his fingers in the palm of his hand and looked at Zora. "I guess there's no time like the present to try to master this thing." He moved down to the floor and approached the archway. "Shift away from Black Frost, Tatiana. I want to focus on a smaller target."

"Certainly."

The image moved off the enormous form of Black Frost and zeroed in on a pair of Riskers riding side by side on grand dragons.

Something stirred in Grey Cloak's mind. His wizard fire ignited and connected with the helmet, and a vibrant awakening expanded his mind. He, the helm, and his wizardry were one. He set his eyes on the dragons in the sky and touched their thoughts.

"I can feel them." Grey Cloak wandered closer to the archway. "They tire and are hungry, but are loyal to the death."

He forced his thoughts on one of the dragons. It surged ahead, slowed down, then drifted back alongside the other.

"Did you do that?" Dyphestive asked.

Grey Cloak smirked. "I did." His knees wobbled, and his head throbbed all over. "Whoa."

Zora ran to his side and steadied him. "What's wrong?"

"The helm—it's reaching out to more dragons, picking at their minds. It... wants to control them all."

Zora squeezed his waist. "I told you it has a mind of its own."

Grey Cloak's jaw hung open as blood-hungry thoughts started to enter his mind. "I feel like I'm in a crowded room, and everyone is talking at once." His eyes squeezed shut as the desires of scores of dragons weighed upon him. "They are devoted. They seek death. With Black Frost, they feel invincible."

"Those Riskers aren't the problem. We can fend them off. It's Black Frost we can't deal with," Tatianna said. "Perhaps you can use them against him."

"Not yet." Grey Cloak spread his arms out at his sides. "I need to work with them."

The dragons were following the same simple command. Escort Black Frost to the Wizard Watch. Attack as ordered. Kill any enemy in sight.

"Hmm... I've connected with all of them." Grey Cloak pointed at the mural. "Tatiana, move the image back. You'll notice the dragons fly in V formation above Black Frost, excluding the scouts that are ahead. The leader might be the distraction we need. They'll follow him."

"I thought they followed Black Frost," Zora said.

"Oh, they do, but he doesn't command them directly." Grey Cloak used the Dragon Helm to carefully slip into the minds of all the other dragons. It was like addressing the room of a captive audience. His thoughts worked with theirs, already executing his plan. "I've used a back door to sneak into their heads. I've gained their confidence. This should be interesting."

Dyphestive joined his brother's side and looked over to Tatiana. "How close are they?"

"They are beyond those hills. We'll be able to see them with the naked eye at any moment."

She panned the image all the way back to the tower view.

"Grey Cloak, are you still in contact, or do I need to pull them into view?"

"I have contact."

Silence fell over the chamber as everyone watched the mural.

"I can feel my heartbeat in my ears," Zora said quietly.

The thunder of dragons appeared beneath the clouds like a flock of birds cruising the sky. They appeared small and harmless at first then grew into a menacing threat of claws and scales. Black Frost, a great behemoth in the air, hovered beneath them like a flying hunk of land. He passed over the hilltops, spread out his expansive wings, then pulled up. As he landed, great trees snapped like twigs underneath his girth. He waded through the woodland on two feet, his head far above the canopy of trees.

"He's too big for this world," Dyphestive said. "How are we going to stop something like that?"

"Do you want me to fire up the mystic cannons?" Nath asked.

"No," Grey Cloak quickly replied. "Let him think the tower is dormant." He smirked. "I don't want him to see what's coming."

The thunder of dragons split into separate formations. One V rounded the tower. The other circled above Black Frost.

Zora tightened her grip around his waist. "I don't know what you are planning, but you better do it soon."

"We are safe one way or the other," Tatiana said. "Even if the tower falls, we are still far away in the south."

Zora squeezed Grey Cloak's hand.

Black Frost was no more than a few strides away. The cracks

between his chest scales heated up. His blazing eyes became great blue pits of fire.

Grey Cloak envisioned what he wanted to happen and targeted Black Frost. He planted a seed in the dragons' minds of Black Frost being a huge dragon with golden scales, ridden by a huge Sky Rider.

Then he unleashed his mental command. *Dragons, attack!*

21

Black Frost's dragon escort swarmed him. They dive-bombed the gargantuan dragon, hitting him at full speed, then latched on to his scales.

There was no mistaking the shocked look on the Riskers' faces. They pulled on their reins and kicked their heels into their dragons' ribs.

Dragon fire spewed, and claws ripped into scales and dug for flesh. They frenzied, tearing at Black Frost's wings and piercing him from all directions.

The Helm of the Dragons throbbed on Grey Cloak's head. He soaked in the dragons' bloodlust and new strength flowed through him. He pushed his illusion deeper into the dragons' minds. The more he focused, the more they fought. They became one with him, sharing his single thought.

"Grey Cloak!" Zora shouted. "What are you doing?"

Her voice was distant. Shallow. Drowned out by blood rushing through ears. His jaws clenched. He wanted to fight. His primal instincts were ready to destroy. The elf's subconscious was being buried.

A pulse of energy, like the sting of a bee, shot through his limbs. The Cloak of Legends woke his good senses. *That's not the plan.*

The image in the archway showed an irritated Black Frost shedding the army from his body. His brow was knitted together. Fire streamed from his mouth, engulfing him and the flames that raked from his body.

Grey Cloak's first command had done its job. He'd duped the enemy dragons with a strong suggestion and illusion. His gaze set upon Black Frost.

Now is the time to find a doorway into your skull, Immense One.

He sharpened his thoughts to the point of a spear, pulled his command from the dragons, then attacked the agitated mind of Black Frost. He probed the mental barrier of the overlord, searching for a crease or a crack in the wall. Wherever he probed, the mental shield strengthened. Grey Cloak persisted. *Everything has a weakness.*

He nudged and nicked, gently seeking out a soft spot in the monster's iron will. But the fence became stronger. *Impossible! Everyone has limitations.*

"Black Frost is brushing away his forces," Dyphestive said urgently. "They are breaking off their attack and beginning to regroup."

Grey Cloak watched the entire event unfold in the mural. Then he squeezed his eyes shut. *Focus! Find that opening.*

Like a woodpecker, he pecked all over Black Frost's mental defenses. Moving from spot to spot, at the speed of thought, he finally uncovered a weakness—a distracted area in the recesses of Black Frost's mind revealed a small gap.

That's it! Grey Cloak used his thoughts like a lance and plunged in. Immediately, he felt the everlasting burning hatred of Black Frost's mind. Inside was a hunger that could not be satisfied.

Zooks! Instinctively, Black Frost pushed back against the forceful mind attack of the Helm of the Dragons. Grey Cloak staggered where he stood. *No, I'm too close!*

He summoned all of his mental fortitude and shoved back with his full might. A single simple command crossed his mind. *Rest!*

Black Frost's mind went blank.

The Helm of the Dragons turned into a boiling pot on Grey Cloak's head. He tore it off and flung it away. It skidded across the floor and butted up against the wall. The dragon charms burned like stars. Their scintillating light began to fade and cool.

He blew on his fingertips. His cheeks were red from the metal's hot touch.

"My skull almost caught fire." Grey Cloak fought to keep his footing.

Zora steadied him. She blinked and rubbed her eyes. "The helm nearly blinded us. I never felt power like that. I thought we'd be consumed."

Sweat dripped from Tatiana's chin. Gossamer's face was beaded with sweat too.

Grey Cloak rubbed his temples and rolled his jaw. "I feel like my head's been in an oven and a meat grinder." He eyed the Helm of the Dragons in the corner. "It worked, I think."

As the burning light of the helmet cooled, its dragon charms started to fall off.

"Anvils!" Dyphestive rushed over to the helmet and reached for it. The skin of his fingers sizzled when he touched it. "Hot as a furnace."

Instead, Dyphestive picked up one of the stones that had fallen on the floor. It crumbled in his hand. "It's broken."

Zora pointed at the mural. "Look!"

Everyone's heads turned toward the image.

Black Frost's eyes were closed, and his wings were folded over his back. His body swayed on the girth of his sturdy legs.

"What command did you execute?" Tatiana asked.

"Rest," Grey Cloak answered. "I wanted it to be short and clear. It couldn't be a word that would be jarring. I imagined, even with his might, he would be worn down. He'd have to be after using all of his energy, not only on himself but on the others."

Tatiana managed an approving smile.

From his pewter seat, Nath said, "I think you made a wise choice. The question is, how long will it last?"

The Riskers hovered with uncertain faces before they landed on the overlord. Hesitant and wide-eyed, they began poking and prodding him with weapons with magic tips. Black Frost didn't budge.

"Well done, brother. You've bought us more time." Dyphestive stood behind him and rubbed Grey Cloak's shoulders. "Now we have a perfect opportunity to kill him."

Grey Cloak nodded. "How do you suppose we do that?"

"We'll think of something." Dyphestive shrugged and said to the group, "But we better act quick. I doubt he'll rest forever, especially with the Riskers trying to wake him."

22

Dyphestive scooped up the Helm of the Dragons and held a few more of its dragon charms in place. He took the loose stones and dropped them into the bowl of the helmet. Looking to the sorceress, he said, "Can it be repaired?"

"It's no short matter of time, but it's possible." Tatiana crossed the room and took the helmet from him. She fished through the charms inside. "Their power has been exhausted. Not in all cases, but some. The stones are drained. We'd need more to rebuild the helm's power."

Zora opened up Crane's satchel. She fished out a dragon charm. "I have one."

"I have a couple too." Grey Cloak rummaged through his inner pockets and produced an emerald- and ruby-colored dragon charm. Like Zora, he dropped them in the helmet.

Tatiana held up the dragon helm and traced the scorch

marks on the metal with her fingers. A crack ran through the top of the helm to the back. "The damage is worse than I thought. We might have to use another helm entirely."

"I don't think the helm needs to be our focus," Gossamer said. "If there is a way to strike down Black Frost, we need to try it now." He pointed at the monstrous dragon's image in the archway. "The Riskers gather and protect his weak spots. Every orifice is guarded. His nostrils, mouth, and earholes are covered. A man could walk through the nostrils like a cave, but the earholes are still tiny. If Black Frost's grey matter could be accessed, we could do a great deal of damage. Possibly even kill him."

Grey Cloak's eyes lit up. He retrieved the Stone of Transport from his pocket. "I like the way you think." He searched the wizards' faces. "What sort of weapon do we have that can do enough damage?"

"Black Frost's skull is enormous." Dalsay moved back behind the pedestal and panned the image back so only Black Frost's head showed. Riskers on grands, two abreast, were perched comfortably between the dragon overlord's horns. "In the Treasure House of the Vault of the Wizards, there is a creation, an explosive device. It can do a great deal of harm."

"The Orb of Devastation," Gossamer said.

Dalsay nodded.

"What are we waiting for?" Grey Cloak responded. "Let's go fetch this orb."

Along with Gossamer, Zora, and Dyphestive, Grey Cloak stood inside the Treasure House looking at the Orb of Devastation. "It's not exactly portable, is it?"

The orb was a huge seamless hunk of black steel the size of a barrel of ale. It sat on a custom-crafted wooden rack like the bell of a goblet, hanging halfway off.

Grey Cloak stretched out his hand. "Can I touch it?"

"Certainly." Gossamer pushed the sleeves on his robes above his elbows. "It takes a wizard to activate it."

Grey Cloak's fingers dusted over the smooth metal surface. There were circles spaced out evenly all over the ball. "What are these rings?"

"When the orb is activated, spikes come out, fixing it to its target." Gossamer pointed to a lone red circle among the others. "Press this to activate the spike and plant the orb. Very simple. We can trigger it from a distance if need be, but it will explode on its own after a minute. So don't delay. Once activated, it won't deactivate."

Grey Cloak exchanged an uncomfortable look with Zora and Dyphestive. "Sounds nasty. But how am I supposed to carry this out of here? It must be heavy."

Dyphestive reached into the custom rack and hoisted up the orb with a grunt. "Uh, heavy like an anvil. Heavier actually." With the orb scooped up in his muscular arms, he said, "What are we waiting for? Let's invade the dragon's nostril."

"You don't have to do this," Grey Cloak said.

"I don't think we have a choice. You can't lift this." Dyphestive raised an eyebrow and looked at Gossamer. "And if you can't lift this, I don't see how a wizard could."

"Oh, we don't lift heavy objects with our arms," Gossamer stated matter-of-factly. He wiggled his fingers. "We use our wizardry to do that."

They returned to the Time Mural chamber, Dyphestive lugging the orb the whole way.

"Black Frost hasn't moved," Tatiana said, "but if you watch, you'll see his scales twitch." She zoomed the image in on Black Frost's nostrils. A Risker in a full-metal dragon suit of armor stood at the entrance of each one. "You'll have to teleport behind them. And remember, we can't see what you are doing inside. Once you teleport back, we'll activate it. And beware, Black Frost's flames can spill through his nostrils."

With the Rod of Weapons tucked under one arm, Grey Cloak grabbed Dyphestive with one hand and held the Stone of Transport in the other. He stared at the spot in the dragon's nostril where he wanted to travel. "Here we go, brother. Hang on."

They vanished.

Zora watched the archway, holding her elbows. She felt like she was standing on pins and needles. "I don't like this."

Tatiana joined her. "It's a sound plan. Dangerous but sound. I've come to have faith in our friends. They are remarkable people."

"Agreed," Zanna said.

"I know. But planting the orb in that's monster's skull? Look at him. It will be a journey, and how will they know where they are going?" Zora picked her lips. "Not to mention being disgusting. I have goosebumps all over."

Tatiana put her arm around her friend's waist. "I don't know, but we can only hope that they find a way like they always do. They have a knack for it."

Zora nodded. "Do you really think the Orb of Devastation is strong enough to kill Black Frost?"

"We'll find out soon enough."

Zora saw Black Frost's eyelids twitch. Chills ran down her spine. "Did you see that?"

"I did," Tatiana replied.

"Oh no." Zora gasped. Both of Black Frost's eyes opened up. "He's awake."

23

Grey Cloak and Dyphestive appeared about two horse lengths deep inside the gooey cavern of Black Frost's nostril.

Dyphestive started to open his mouth, but Grey Cloak clamped his hand over his brother's mouth. He pointed toward the light at the end of the tunnel. A Risker stood with his back to the entrance.

With a nod, Dyphestive stooped over and waddled—orb in arms—deeper into Black Frost's cavity.

Another dozen or more feet in, Grey Cloak ignited the Rod of Weapons and moved to the front. "Follow me," he said in a hushed voice.

The tunnel inside the monster's skull smelled of brimstone and sulfur. The soft, squishy ground shifted underfoot. Grey Cloak and his brother climbed, venturing farther into Black Frost's head.

"How do we know we are on the right path?" Dyphestive whispered.

"We can't be certain, but the dragon's snout should lead into the back of his skull." Grey Cloak knew more about dragon anatomy than himself—he'd studied as much in Hidemark when he'd trained to be a Sky Rider. He'd never dissected a dragon, but he knew where they had weaknesses and where their fire came from. "How are you holding up?"

Dyphestive's bare arms were layered in sweat, and his damp hair was matted to his head. He kept shifting the orb in his arms, fighting for a better grip. "It's steamy in here, and the orb's slick as a greasy pig."

"Can you handle it?"

"I'll be fine. Looking back, I probably should have brought a sack or blanket. Keep going." He nudged his brother from behind. "I'll make it."

"Well, if you had a cloak like mine, you wouldn't have to worry about it." He came to a stop where the cavity made a sudden drop. "Huh, it looks like that might be his throat. Straight down to the belly." He squatted and leaned over the fleshy pit. "Maybe we should drop the orb in there?"

"I like the idea of destroying his mind better." Dyphestive shifted the orb in his arms again and eyed the two cavities above the pit. "The grey matter must be that way."

There was a narrow ledge around the pit of the throat.

Grey Cloak spied the area and rubbed his chin. "Your boots are bigger than that lip. I don't think you can make it any farther."

"I can make it." The orb slipped in Dyphestive's arms. "Trust me."

"If you fall into his belly, I'm not getting you out."

"Sure you will." Dyphestive edged toward the lip. With his back to the fleshy wall, he started to amble toward the pit. The orb slipped in his arms. He caught it on his knees. "Not good."

Grey Cloak had an epiphany. He removed his cloak. "Wrap it up in this."

Dyphestive's eyes brightened. "Ha, a fine idea, brother." He bundled up the orb. "Much better."

"Ugh!" Grey Cloak's clothing steamed up and clung to his body, suddenly wet. "I'm sweating." He looked at the arms of his damp shirt. "Profusely." He shoved Dyphestive toward the ledge. "Let's get this over with."

Dyphestive shuffled up the ledge toward the above cavities with Grey Cloak close behind him.

The entire chamber shook. More steam started to rise from Black Frost's gullet.

"I hope that isn't what I think it is." Grey Cloak looked down into the pit. Deep down, a cauldron of blue flames started to churn. He pushed his brother. "He's awake. Go, go, go!"

"Do you really think so? Maybe he's snoring?" Dyphestive said as he picked up the pace.

Grey Cloak pushed him along. "And maybe he isn't. If he breathes, we'll be turned into ash, and I don't have my cloak on. Move it, brother, move it."

"I'm moving. I'm moving." With the orb balled up in the cloak as a makeshift sack, he slung it over his back and sank his fingers into the fleshy wall. He climbed up into the next cavity, reached back, and offered his hand to his brother.

Without any assistance, Grey Cloak joined his brother in the upper cavity. He wiped his damp hair from his eyes. "Is it me, or is it getting hotter?"

"It's getting hotter."

"I have a feeling Black Frost is about to blow!" He shoved his brother in the backside. "Go! Go! Go!"

"I don't know where I'm going."

"It doesn't matter. Go as far back as you can! And don't stop until you hit grey matter."

They made it another thirty paces then hit a wall with tiny holes in it.

Grey Cloak ran his fingers over the porous surface. "I think this is bone. Zooks. And a dead end." He looked high and low." The cavity was as solid as stone walls. "He's a fortress inside and out."

The heat started to rise. The tunnel behind them began to brighten.

"Take out the orb. This is as far as we are going to get."

Dyphestive set down the orb. "Maybe I can bust through it. Give me a chance."

"There's no time. We're about to be scorched alive." He unwrapped the orb and slung his cloak over his shoulders. His body cooled. "Ah, that's better." He rolled the orb against the wall and pressed the red ring that Gossamer had pointed out.

Spikes popped out and buried themselves into the dragon's

inner walls of flesh like a bur. Dyphestive gave it an additional shove, driving it to the bone.

Black Frost's body—awakening with life—moaned. The floor quaked underneath their feet. Flames began to rise in the cavities behind them. The hot, suffocating air surrounded them.

Grey Cloak hooked his brother's arm, envisioned the Time Mural chamber, and ignited the Stone of Transport's power.

In the nick of time, they reappeared in the center of the chamber.

Zora hopped up like a frightened bunny and squealed. "You scared the skin off me!"

"Sorry." Grey Cloak brushed the sweat from his brow with his thumb. He searched out Gossamer and said, "The Orb of Devastation is planted. Trigger it."

Gossamer passed his hands through the air, but nothing happened. "Are you sure that you activated it?"

"Positive. The spikes came out, and we lodged it in the canal, but I don't know that we made it deep enough." Grey Cloak studied the image in the mural. "Look! What are they doing?"

Two Riskers ducked into Black Frost's nasal cavity.

"Horseshoes!" Dyphestive paled as he watched through the archway. "They must be going after that orb. They are going to dig it out."

"Gossamer, why isn't it working?" Grey Cloak clenched his fists.

The elven wizard shrugged. "I don't know."

24

Grey Cloak stood staring in disbelief at Gossamer. "What do you mean, you don't know?"

"Black Frost's power is so vast, perhaps he negated it, or the orb is not functional. These matters happen with magic. Sometimes, it works. Sometimes, not. After all, the orb was made centuries ago and never used."

"You're telling me that we risked our lives planting a device that might not work?"

"The Orb of Devastation was a safety measure placed in the Treasure Room in case the towers were ever invaded." Gossamer continued to massage the air in an effort to activate the orb from afar. "It would destroy the room and everything in it, including the tower."

Grey Cloak tilted back his head and sighed. "And I had to get sweaty for nothing."

"Brother, look." Dyphestive beckoned him toward the mural.

Black Frost pointed a claw at the tower. When he spoke, his booming voice carried from the wilds through the walls of the tower where the heroes stood. "I know what you've done. I can sense it." His blue eyes burned like the sun. "I will undo it. I am Black Frost, and no mortal weapon can defeat—"

Booom!

The Wizard Watch shook from top to bottom. Everyone inside stumbled over their feet.

Tatiana fell at the base of the pedestal, as did Gossamer. Grey Cloak steadied Zora, and together, they watched the image in the archway cloud up and blur.

"What happened? Get the image back!" Grey Cloak said.

Tatiana grabbed the rim of the Pedestal of Power and hauled herself up to her feet. "Give me a moment, and I'll have the image restored."

Everyone exchanged nervous glances. Grey Cloak didn't know whether Black Frost had struck or whether the Orb of Devastation had ignited. The smoky image in the mural began to sharpen, then he got his answer. "Whoa."

Black Frost stood on two legs, swaying side to side. A gaping, smoking hole was between his snout and right eye socket. The eyeball had been completely blown out, and a huge hunk of the dragon's snout was gone, forming an ugly, deformed cavity.

Smoke and blue flames spewed out of the ugly fissure of charred and torn-up scales.

"Rogues of Rodden!" Zora exclaimed. "He's falling!"

As she said it, Black Frost toppled like a mighty oak and crashed into the earth on his right side. *Thud!*

The tower trembled for a moment. A quiet followed.

The Riskers couldn't hide the shocked looks on their faces. Jaws hung wide open. Some even teared up. Most of them landed at the body of their lord and master. Others wailed and shook their fists at the tower with rage.

"Did we kill him?" Grey Cloak asked his friends.

Everyone in the room exchanged equally perplexed looks. Even Nath was on the edge of his seat, his golden eyes wide.

Grey Cloak's heartbeat raced in his ears. Black Frost lay as prone as a petrified log.

For the longest time, no one said anything. All of them stared at the fallen monster as if waiting for him to stir at any moment. Even the smoke and fire emanating from Black Frost's exploded eye socket dwindled.

All of the heroes gathered in front of the mural and stood side by side.

"He's dead," Dyphestive muttered. "I think he's dead."

Outside, on the grounds where Black Frost had fallen, the Riskers and their dragons nudged the tremendous monster with horns and spears, trying to get a spark out of him.

Black Frost's chest didn't rise or fall.

A towering Risker, along with others, pressed his ear against Black Frost's chest. They backed away, heads shaking, despair filling their faces. Many of them sank to their knees and wailed like children. The dragons let out frightening roars filled with agony.

"We did it." Grey Cloak spoke feebly, but his voice grew stronger. "We did it." He grabbed Zora by the waist, hoisted her up, and swung her around like a child. "We did it! He's dead! Ha ha! Can you believe it?"

Everyone's nervous smiles became the real thing. All of the friends hugged and shook hands with one another.

The blood brothers embraced. Zanna hugged Zora and Tatiana.

"Sweet potatoes! We did it, brother!" Dyphestive spread out his arms and let out a gusty laugh. "The war is over!"

Grey Cloak caught Nath's slight smile out of the corner of his eye. "Nath, we can send you home now. Your world will be saved, won't it?"

Nath combed his fingers through his long strands of hair. "That's what I would think, but I don't feel anything."

"What do you mean?" Grey Cloak asked. "We'll return you to the portal at Dark Mountain and send you back to the world you came from." He gave Tatiana an excited look. "Or we can send you back from here, possibly?"

With a beautiful smile on her face, she replied, "The future is filled with possibilities."

Everyone faced Nath, who stood on the throne's platform.

"What did you think would happen when Black Frost perished?" Dyphestive asked.

"I thought the energy stolen from Nalzambor would flow back into me," Nath replied. "But I feel as weak as ever." He pulled his hunched shoulders back, and his golden eyes grew like saucers. "Egads, I fear we began our celebration too early. Look."

Everyone spun around and faced the mural. Inside, the Riskers started to cheer like wild men. Dragons roared like thunder in the wind.

Black Frost opened his one good eye. He pushed up off the ground and started to rise.

Grey Cloak's blood sank into his toes as his heart deflated. "Zooks."

25

Black Frost wasted no time destroying the Wizard Watch in Arrowwood. From the southernmost Wizard Watch, in the safety of the Time Mural chamber, Grey Cloak and company watched it happen. Grey Cloak paced with his hands behind his back.

"I think he's mad," Nath said from his chair, his chin propped on his hands. "I'd be upset, too, if you took out a hunk of my face. Impressive though. He's begun healing, but don't worry. I think a lot of the damage will be permanent."

Tatiana lay over the Pedestal of Power, her robes drenched in sweat.

Dalsay tried to rest his ghostly hand on her back. "You need rest, love. When the tower is drained, you are as well. Trying to shield the tower from destruction is too much. His strength is too great. Once a tower is lost, it is lost. The Time Mural with it. Save your energy to defend the last one."

Tatiana raised her sagging head. "You're right. We need to pool all of our resources into the tower in Crow Valley." She spread out her hands on the rim of the pedestal. "This tower will be lost the moment he arrives."

"What are you saying?" Zora asked.

"She's saying we need to abandon this tower. Let Black Frost take it without a fight." He looked at the stones in the archway. He could still see Black Frost's seething expression. The dragon overlord was furious, and he wouldn't hesitate to take down the next tower he struck. "But we can't make it that easy on him. We need to show some sort of defense. If anything, it will buy time."

"I don't disagree, but when I say we need to save our energy, I mean we need every bit." Tatiana shook her head. "If the last tower falls, we are all lost."

"Are there any more Orbs of Devastation stowed away in your secret lair?" Dyphestive asked. "Perhaps we can turn the tower into a trap. Once Black Frost attacks—" He clapped his hands together. "Boom!"

"The Orb of Devastation was the most powerful weapon we had, but I do like the way you think." Gossamer looked at Tatiana. "It is possible to plant a Shield of Destruction in the tower while we watch from the safety of Crow Valley."

Dalsay nodded and stroked his beard. "Between the three of us, we can build a seed before Black Frost arrives." His glance shifted over to Nath. "We'll need you to manage the mystic cannons."

Nath grinned. "It would be my pleasure."

Grey Cloak flipped the Rod of Weapons around. "I don't know what a Shield of Destruction is, but it sounds better than rolling over to that beast. We'll return to Dwarf Skull, warn the others, and check Rhonna's progress on the Apparatus of Ruune."

"The final battle is doing to take place at the last tower in Crow Valley," Tatiana said. "We are going to need all of the forces we can muster to keep Black Frost away from it."

"Yes, well, let's hope the artifact is ready by then." He handed Zora the Rod of Weapons. "Hold this, if you will." He grabbed her and Dyphestive by the wrists and said to his mother, Zanna, "I'll be back for you."

Zanna nodded. "No rush. I'm sure I can be of assistance here."

He nodded. "Time to go."

The trio vanished and reappeared in the streets of Dwarf Skull near the armory.

Crane, Gorva, Razor, and Shannon were sitting on the walkway, playing cards. The old man spotted the new arrivals first. "Look who's back!"

Grey Cloak made his way over to them. "Any news from Rhonna?"

Razor shook his head. "The place has been sealed up like a drum." He tossed down his hand of bird cards and stood. "Any good news on your end?"

"Well, we blew half of Black Frost's face off using the Orb of Devastation."

"What?" Gorva jumped to her feet and grabbed him by the cloak. "Tell me about that orb. Do we have more of them? Is Black Frost dead?"

Dyphestive answered, "We dropped him like an anvil. I swear he died, but he climbed back to his feet angrier than ever."

Gorva grunted. She released Grey Cloak. "So, he lives. What of the towers?"

"They are all gone except the one in the south and Crow Valley. Black Frost moves fast, and he'll have the southern Wizard Watch down in a day. Then he'll be coming here." Grey Cloak looked at the armory's closed door. "I don't know when that weapon will be ready, but we have to keep Black Frost away from the last tower at all costs. If he destroys them all, according to Tatiana, all hope for Gapoli will be lost."

"Not if we still have the weapon, right?"

"If the tower falls, it's only a matter of hours before all of Dwarf Skull is destroyed." Grey Cloak moved to the door and put his hands on it.

I should teleport in. She'll never know.

A heavy hand squeezed his shoulder. "I know what you're thinking, brother," Dyphestive said. "Don't do it. We need to have faith. Trust Rhonna."

"I was only going to take a peek."

At that moment, the armory doors cracked open. A sweaty Lythlenion, wearing a black armor apron, stepped out and closed the doors behind him. He wiped his arm across his forehead and dabbed a blue handkerchief over his face.

"Is it finished?" Grey Cloak asked.

Lythlenion shook his head. "They have a long way to go."

"Then what are you doing here?"

Lythlenion shrugged. "They kicked me out. Said I was slowing them down." He took a deep breath and stretched his spine. "The truth is, I'm relieved. They were breaking my back. Perhaps it's my age." He looked between Grey Cloak and Dyphestive. "So, what is going on in the real world?"

In unison, the Blood Brothers said, "You don't want to know."

26

Dwarf Skull's forces marched out of the city toward Crow Valley. Horses brought up the rear, towing siege machines behind them. The dwarves numbered in the thousands and moved at a brisk pace.

Grey Cloak stood on the city's wall, looking between the battlements with Gorva and Dyphestive. "I don't know whether they'll make it there in time."

"No, but we have to try," Dyphestive said. "We know that we can wound Black Frost. If we can get him down on the ground again, we might have a chance."

"It's a good plan, but it won't be easy. Black Frost has more Riskers than we have dragons," Grey Cloak said. "They'll be protecting him from our attacks on his wings. If we can't get him to the ground, he'll pick the tower apart from above."

"I don't know about that." Dyphestive rubbed his chin. "He's attacked with his feet planted every time. What makes you think he'll change his tactic?"

"He's not overconfident now that we hurt him. He'll exercise more caution. I would, wouldn't you?"

Gorva nodded. "Agreed. You say we need more forces in the air? We might have an ally if you'll take me there."

Grey Cloak tilted his head. "Who are you talking about?"

"Jumax. Leader of the Sky Gnomes who call themselves the Southern Storm. They are south of Crow Valley."

"And what makes you think they'll help?"

"It never hurts to ask. Besides, he likes me."

"That's a sound enough reason for me." He took out the emerald-colored Stone of Transport, placed it in her palms, then closed both of his hands over hers. "I don't know where we are going. You'll have to take us there. All you need to do is close your eyes, picture where you want to go, and concentrate."

Thrust through time and space, they appeared inside a cave in the rocky spires of the Sky Gnome's home.

A bald, aging gnome with oversized features jumped off of his stool and dropped a bowl of porridge. He clutched at his heart, his bulging eyes blinking. "Gorva! Is that you? Where in the heavens did you come from?" He eyed Grey Cloak. "And who is this elf I see?"

"Durmost, this is my comrade, Grey Cloak, a true friend." She released the stone to Grey Cloak, who quickly hid it in his pocket. "It's urgent that I talk to Jumax. We need his help."

Durmost bent over and picked up his bowl. "We? How so?"

"Black Frost and his forces will be invading Crow Valley any day now. He comes to destroy the last tower of the Wizard Watch. Once it goes, chaos will fall with it. He'll wipe out anyone that is not loyal to him."

Durmost set his bowl on a shelf. "It's not likely that Black Frost will trouble us. There is little for us to fear this far south, aside from the lizardmen." He winked at Gorva. "But you helped us take care of that."

Gorva moved in front of the gnome and took a knee. She grabbed his arm gently and said, "Please, Durmost, summon him. I would not have come if it wasn't urgent. Your people are in grave danger. All of us are."

Durmost blinked his bulging eyes a few more times, and his cheeks flushed red. He patted her hand. "Though Jumax does not like to be disturbed, for you, I will do it. But you owe me. Wait here."

The sky gnome hurried from his humble abode out onto the overlook, took some rough-hewn steps up, then disappeared.

Grey Cloak followed him outside and took in the odd landscape of rocky spires, which climbed straight up for hundreds of feet. Huge vultures flew between the pinnacles and perched in the rocks. Some of them had gnome riders. "I've never imagined such a place. It's fantastic in its own beautiful way. I can see why they feel they are safe, but Black Frost would knock these rocks down like game tiles."

Gorva joined him. "Agreed. I would think dragons would like it, but to my surprise, they are not here. Instead, vultures."

"And gnomes." Grey Cloak checked his pocket for the Stone of Transport and squeezed it in his grip. "I've lost some of my affection for gnomes recently. So, tell me about Jumax. You speak fondly of him."

With her chin jutted out, Gorva made a slight smile. "He's an impressive person. I think you'll like him."

"He's a gnome?"

"No, but you'll see. I think he's very big on first impressions." She searched the skies.

"Does he look like a vulture? Perhaps he can turn into one?"

Durmost reappeared, hopping down from another set of stairs on the other side. "I have sent a message to him." He stood in front of Gorva and followed her gaze skyward. "He comes. Be patient."

Grey Cloak checked his nails, which were filled with grit. He reached for one of his daggers. "Let me know when you see Jumax. In the meantime, I'll make myself presentable." He began cleaning his fingernails.

27

"There he is! There he is!" Durmost teetered back and forth on his feet in a little dance. He pointed high in the sky. "Do you see him?"

Grey Cloak slid his dagger back into his sheath and spotted the figure of a man dropping from beneath the clouds. "He can fly?"

"He can do anything," Durmost replied.

Gorva's face, which normally wore a grim look or a frown, held a rare smile. There was no mistaking the brightness in her eyes.

Jumax dove toward their overlook headfirst, his body corkscrewing on the way down. All of a sudden, his arms spread out like an eagle's wings. Plumes of feathers running along his arms fanned out. He pulled up, head raising toward the sky, then hovered with his winged arms beating, the sun and clouds behind his back.

"I am Jumax. Who summons me?" he said in a loud and rich voice.

Gorva waved her arm.

Jumax floated down toward their position with a radiant smile growing on his face. He landed softly in front of Gorva. "My love!" He took her hand in his and kissed it. "I have missed you so!"

"My love?" Grey Cloak muttered. He scratched his head as he studied the strange winged natural.

Jumax was bald as an egg with striking hawkish good looks. His body was chiseled with muscles, sculpted to perfection. Sun-browned skin highlighted his flawless frame. A large knife hung from a leather belt, and a skirt of feathers half covered his powerful legs. For a natural, he was a specimen among specimens, standing taller than them all.

"It's good to see you." Gorva received his embrace and made no effort to break it, closing her eyes and resting her head on the hardened muscles of his broad chest. She appeared to lose herself for a moment, but when she opened her eyes and spotted Grey Cloak smirking at her, she began to pull away. "Jumax, we need your help."

"We, eh?" Jumax looked over at Grey Cloak. "We being you and your little elf friend?"

"His name is Grey Cloak. He brought me here."

"Grey Cloak? You're named after a garment? How odd."

Jumax put his arm over Gorva's shoulder and led her inside Durmost's abode. "Tell me more about your troubles."

Gorva spent a great deal of time explaining the recent incidents with Black Frost and the Wizard Watch. Jumax soaked in her words.

When she finished, he said, "I will help you, but you must become my queen when it is over."

"*Queen?*" Grey Cloak exclaimed.

Gorva glared at him. Then she turned her attention back to Jumax. "You know that I am fond of you, but I cannot make such a promise... at this time."

"Ah. Jumax does not like your answer, but he will accept it," Jumax said. "But no woman has ruffled my feathers like you. You are incredible. A woman born to rule by my side." He kissed her hand. "However, I want to see Black Frost in person. I will escort my scouts, and we will weigh the graveness of this threat. In the meantime, please make yourself at home, and be my most welcome guests."

Grey Cloak cleared his throat. "As much of an honor that might be, we need to return back to Dwarf Skull and continue preparations."

Jumax raised an eyebrow. "That is disappointing."

"As a sign of good faith, I will stay," Gorva said.

"What?" Grey Cloak couldn't hide his shock. "I don't think that is a good—"

"It is decided then!" Jumax said with a broad smile. "Grey Garment, return to your people. Tell them Jumax, leader of the Southern Storm, will look into things."

"What do you mean, Gorva wanted to stay?" Razor said in a huff.

They were inside a dwarven mead hall filled with long wooden tables, benches, and more barrels of ale stacked against the walls than they had time to count. The vaulted ceiling above was supported by wooden beams.

"It's a sign of good faith," Grey Cloak replied. "Jumax commands a formidable army, and we'll need their assistance to slow Black Frost. Gorva has a past relationship—"

"Oh, I know they had a past relationship." Razor hit his chest with his fist. "I was there. I met that glorious specimen of a human." He picked up a tankard of ale and guzzled it halfway down. "Is Jumax still bald?"

"Bald as a river rock," he assured him.

Razor combed his full head of hair back with his fingers. "Good."

Zora giggled, and Shannon, who was sitting down beside her, laughed with her.

"Somebody is jealous." Shannon sawed her knife into a hunk of ham then ran it through a pile of mash potatoes on her plate. She looked at Grey Cloak. "Tell us more about Jumax. He sounds"—she toyed with her hair—"intriguing."

"He has feathers on his arms like a bird," Razor fired back. "And a big nose."

"Hmph." Zora turned around on the bench and leaned back against the table. "What about the rest of him?"

"Why don't you wait and see for yourself?" Razor paced the floor, his hands twisting on the pommels of his hip blades. "Stupid bird man. Trying to seduce my lady. I'll stick it to him."

Dyphestive and Lythlenion entered the mead hall and took a seat behind the table. They watched Razor pace.

"What's the matter with him?" Dyphestive asked.

Grey Cloak pinched his finger and thumb together. "Someone is a wee bit jealous that Gorva remained with Jumax and the Southern Storm."

Dyphestive reached for a bread basket and picked up three fluffy rolls in one hand. He stuffed an entire one in his mouth. "Don't fret it, Reginald," he said between chews. "Gorva is fond of you. Don't get so worked up about it."

"That's easy for you to say. You've never met Jumax." Razor scowled.

"How impressive can he be?" Lythlenion looked to Grey Cloak, who waited for Razor to walk out of earshot before answering.

"Oh, he's pretty impressive."

"I heard that," the blademaster replied.

Grey Cloak shrugged. "I'm going to check on the dragons. Does anyone want to join me?"

Zora stood. "I'll go."

Dyphestive slid her plate of food his way. "Good, then I guess you won't be eating this."

WIZARD WATCH, CROW VALLEY

Zanna sat on the throne platform stairs, trying to set dragon charms into the Helm of the Dragons. One of the stones slipped out of her fingers, but she caught it before it hit the floor.

"You have quick hands." Nath sat down beside her.

"Well, I wish I could get these stones to fit. I feel useless sitting here while they work." Zanna looked at the trio of Tatiana, Gossamer, and Dalsay. The sorcerers encircled the Pedestal of Power, their eyes closed and hands clasped as they mumbled enchanted words.

Nath removed the helmet from Zanna's grasp. "I believe the Helm of the Dragons is toast."

"Toast?"

"It's a modern expression from another world. It means broken." He traced his long fingernails between the dragon charms. "Look at the gems. Do you see how they are cloudy? The shine is gone from them. I fear they are spent."

Zanna sighed. "I suppose it's up to the completion of the Apparatus of Ruune now." She took back the helm and stared into his eyes. "I was raised a Sky Rider. We always thought that we could win every battle in the air. We believed we were invincible. Now there is nothing left of us. And the only protection for this world comes from another one. I have to admit, I never saw any of this coming."

"Evil has a way of slipping by our defenses. Even the best of us. I wouldn't put all of the blame on the Sky Riders. Everyone is responsible for their own actions, no matter how great or how small."

"Thanks for the hermit wisdom."

"You're welcome."

She eyed the lanky hermit, whose scaly skin looked to be slipping from his arms. "I was being sarcastic."

"So was I."

The stone wall inside of the archway began to shift and take form. A clear image of the green hills and snowcapped mountains in the south appeared.

Tatiana opened her eyes. "He comes. The Shield of Destruction is planted." She eyed Nath. "Take your position."

With a groan, Nath stood up. He offered his hand to Zanna, helped her to her feet, then nodded at the thrones. "There are two chairs that can operate the mystic cannons. Why don't you join me? It will be fun."

Zanna eyed the pewter throne. "Why not?" She made herself

comfortable in the chair next to Nath's and fingered the gemstone buttons on the arms. "Interesting."

"We're in the tower in Crow Valley now," Tatiana said as she moved stones in the pedestal around, "but Black Frost is going to the south tower. You'll be fed enough energy to make it interesting, but we have to focus our efforts on the Shield of Destruction. Hopefully, it will supply us with the delay that we need."

Black Frost flew into full view. He came like a dark lord of death, jetting underneath the clouds, escorted by scores of Riskers. The hole in the dragon overlord's face had scarred up, but the ugly jagged orifice remained.

"Tell me, Tatiana, what is the Shield of Destruction designed to do?" Zanna asked. "It seems odd that a shield, which would protect you, could be a damaging force."

"It will protect us, but only momentarily. The shield repels attacks back against the attacker."

"Genius," Nath said. "I like it. Why didn't we use it to destroy Black Frost before?"

"It doesn't reflect the full force of the attack. It absorbs it and turns it back in a concussive wave." Tatiana shrugged. "But there is no way of knowing how it will work against Black Frost's dragon fire. It might work, it might not. We'll see soon enough."

Wings spread wide, Black Frost soared in for a landing a few hundred yards away from the southern tower. His wings folded the moment he landed, and dragons circled his head like a crown. Others flew on and around the tower.

Tatiana's eyebrows knitted together. "Fire at will. Make him as mad as a hornet."

With a little guidance from Nath, it didn't take Zanna long to figure out how to unleash the mystic cannons.

"Ladies first," he said.

"Age before beauty," she answered. "No, I think I'll take the first shot and really stick it to him."

Black Frost marched straight toward the tower.

Zanna's finger depressed the button. A bright torpedo of energy streaked across the sky and hit Black Frost dead center in his massive chest. The spot sizzled, but he didn't slow his steps.

"Well, that was unimpressive. It didn't leave a scratch on him." Zanna pressed another button. "We might as well have poked him with the end of a flaming stick."

"Keep firing," Tatiana ordered. "And focus on him. We want him coming right for the tower."

"Aim for his head," Nath suggested. "That will get his ire up."

The mystic cannons shot out projectile after projectile of energy, striking Black Frost in the face and neck. He waded through the volley of energy like an armored bull walking across a field thick with gnats.

"Is there anything that can slow this monster down?" Zanna asked.

Black Frost walked right up to the tower. The mystic cannons stopped.

"What happened?" Zanna pressed her button repeatedly but nothing happened. "Tatiana!"

"I shut off the cannons. The time has come." Tatiana joined hands around the Pedestal of Power with Gossamer and the ghostly Dalsay. "Brace yourselves, everyone. We're going to feel the impact."

Black Frost's flame came out in a roaring tidal wave of fire.

The cracks between the tower's stones turned bright blue.

With wroth heat permeating the room, Zanna instinctively clutched the arms of the throne.

Thooom! A bright flash shook the entire tower.

Zanna and Nath rocked side to side in their chairs, while Tatiana and Gossamer stumbled to the floor.

Dalsay maintained his suspended position. "I'll bring back the picture."

The mural's image turned fuzzy. The radiant heat in the stone walls cooled. The smoke outside of the tower started to clear. Black Frost loomed over them like a mountainside. A foul snarl was on his face. "I cannot be stopped." His angry voice shook the structure. "And you will all pay for what you did!"

As Tatiana and Gossamer climbed to their feet, Dalsay panned back and scanned the surrounding area. Dozens of Riskers and their dragons lay dead in the open field. The bodies were charred and disfigured. Scales smoked and bodies burned. Wounded dragons and soldiers twitched on the ground.

"Whoa!" Nath said. "We might not have taken him out, but we took out a lot of those Riskers." He gave a thumbs up. "The Shield of Destruction is all right in my book."

Black Frost grabbed the tower in his paws, crushing stone in his grip.

"What's happening?" Zanna asked. "I thought the towers would hold against such physical attacks."

"Our spell drained our defenses," Tatiana said, exhaustion growing on her face. "Dalsay, cut off our connection before he damages the last tower too."

Zanna watched Black Frost throwing huge hunks of stone across the landscape. The fortress began to crumble in a waterfall of debris and dust. The last thing she saw was Black Frost's chest heating up. The fire came. The mural darkened.

Tatiana sagged to the ground and leaned with her back against the pedestal. She dropped her face into her hands. "We are down to the last tower. If he destroys it, he'll control all of the magic left in this world, and nothing will be able to stop him."

"We won't let that happen." Zanna rose from the throne. "Dalsay, pull up an image of our current location."

The wizard nodded. An image of the destitute Crow Valley appeared. The infertile land offered nothing more than a bleak plain of rocks and ridges for leagues all around. But they weren't alone. Dwarven soldiers encamped around the last tower. They were armed to the teeth and working on loading and building up giant siege machines.

Gossamer joined Zanna in front of the archway. "If anyone can slow Black Frost, the dwarves can."

"True," she said, "but it's going to take a lot more than that. We need the Apparatus of Ruune."

29

Grey Cloak and Zora joined the children of Cinder in a shaded climb north of Dwarf Skull. Most of the dragons were curled up against the rocks, some of them resting on top of one another, soaking up the shadows.

A bright-eyed Streak greeted Zora with a lick of his pink tongue while Grey Cloak hugged his bull neck. "It's about time you came to visit. I was about to come and fetch you. Any progress?"

"Not that we know of," Grey Cloak said.

"Huh, that's too bad."

Zora wiped her face with a handkerchief. "No offense, Streak, but you lick like a slobbering hound."

Streak grinned. "I do, don't I?"

Grey Cloak counted the grand dragons sleeping. "Where are the others?"

Streak's twin tails swished across the ground, and he licked underneath his wing. "Anya and Cinder are patrolling the skies. Slick and Slicer are with them." His mighty jaws opened in a yawn. "That woman never rests." With his eyes skyward, he said, "Speak of the devil, here comes Fiery Red."

Shielding their eyes, Grey Cloak and Zora spotted Anya coming in for a landing.

"I don't know why Razor called her that. Her hair is mostly blond," Zora commented.

"Maybe he's color-blind," Streak said.

"Her hair was darker when I trained with her at Hidemark." Grey Cloak looked at Zora's locks. "More auburn like yours. I think all of the time in the sun bleaches it out."

When Cinder landed, his beating wings stirred up the sand, creating small dust devils.

"Speaking of hair," Zora said, "I'm going to have to comb sand out of mine."

Anya was quick to jump out of the saddle. She took off her helmet, and thick layers of white-blond hair fell out. She marched forward with her battle-ravaged armor reflecting the sunlight.

"Grey Cloak, I am glad you are here. I have news to report," the Sky Rider said.

"I take it it's not good news?"

"A large force of the Black Guard marches toward Crow Valley. They are less than a day away," she said.

He sighed. "If it were anyone else, I'd think it was a jest. But it's you, so I know it's true. Are their Riskers among them?"

Anya nodded. "I spotted a dozen."

"Where did they come from?" Zora asked.

"I know where. They are the same troops that were sent south when Gossamer led Black Frost north. We forgot about them." Grey Cloak climbed into Streak's saddle. "We need to warn the dwarves about what is coming. As if Black Frost isn't bad enough, now we have to contend with his minions. It's as if he knew the battle would be there all along."

"That wouldn't surprise me one bit." Anya marched over to the spot where Rock and Snags were sleeping. She kicked Rock in his snout.

The dragon cracked open his eyelid and growled, "Who dares?"

"Nap time is over. Wake up your brothers and sisters. We might have another fight on our hands." Anya stuffed her helmet on and buckled the chin strap. "We'll keep an eye on the enemy. I'll send Slick and Slicer back and forth with their location."

Rock nodded and waved at Cinder. "Don't let her start a war without us."

"I can't promise anything," he replied.

Grey Cloak reached for Zora. "Would you care to fly with me and Streak?"

She took his hand. "I'd love to."

After they doubled up on the saddle, Streak spread out his wings. "Hang on, ladies and gents. It's time to ride the sky!"

30

Night had fallen. Bonfires burned in the dwarven army's camp. Catapults had been assembled and loaded and ballistae mounted in twenty-five-foot towers. Over three thousand dwarven soldiers stood ready to fight. Their leaders met and planned in canvas tents.

Grey Cloak stood on the top of the Wizard Watch overlooking the land. Zora and Streak were with him. He'd met with the dwarven commanders and given them the message. They assured him that they were ready.

The hot desert wind rustled his hair and cloak. Outside of the firelight of the dwarven perimeter was a sea of blackness, nothing but an expansive void on the half-moon night. But it didn't go on forever.

Over a league away, the blackness came to an end. The

rugged hills and flattened plains twinkled from the camps of over six thousand Black Guard soldiers.

Streak stretched his head over the Wizard Watch's pyramid-shaped battlements. "Even if the artifact kills Black Frost, we'll still have a fight on our hands."

"Not if they surrender," Grey Cloak said. "If their leader falls, I imagine they'll fall with him."

"'If' being the question." Zora rummaged through Crane's satchel, took out a vial, and eyed it before putting it back in and closing the flap.

"What's that?" Grey Cloak asked.

"Vitality. I was taking inventory. We only have two left."

"I don't think it's going to matter if we don't win this final fight." Grey Cloak moved from one side of the tower to the other and looked back toward Dwarven Hole, which was too far away to be seen. "We need that contraption. It's our only hope."

"Hope comes from all sorts of unexpected places," she said.

"Where'd you hear that nonsense?"

"Tanlin. I miss him."

Grey Cloak put his hands on her waist. "Well, if we *do* manage to survive, we'll go back to Raven Cliff and see him."

Zora hugged him and laid her head on his chest. "I'd like that."

"Look at those fireworks," Streak said.

"Mind your own business, Streak," Grey Cloak said.

Streak huffed. "I'm not talking about your amorous behavior. I'm talking about the show-offs in the air."

He and Zora looked up in unison. Riskers flew over the black sea, breathing out a challenge of fireballs. They roared and spewed out more streams of flame, but they didn't come within striking range.

"What a bunch of wise guys." Streak breathed out his own flame. "I can't wait to engage. It's going to be nasty."

Slicer and Slick landed on the top of the tower. The slender-built middling dragons huffed for breath. On all fours, they walked over to Streak and bumped horns.

"Hey, brothers," Streak said. "You look tired."

Slicer sat back on his haunches and raked his long claws across each other like a knife on a whetstone. "Big sister Anya sent us east to see whether we could get a fix on Black Frost. We flew our wings off getting there and coming back."

"If it weren't for these harnesses"—Slick scratched under his wing with his back leg like a dog—"we'd have dropped from the sky."

"Did you see him?" Grey Cloak asked.

Slicer replied, "Afraid so. It's hard to miss a mountain in the sky."

"He's a black cloud of doom, he is," Slick added. "But he'll be here soon. I'd say by daybreak."

Grey Cloak punched his palm. "Zooks! How does something so big move so fast?"

"Magic. Like the harnesses, perhaps," Streak suggested.

"Black Frost has powers we can't even imagine. I wonder whether Tatiana has seen this." Grey Cloak took Zora by the hand. "Dragons, stay here. We'll be back."

They teleported inside the Time Mural chamber in front of the archway.

Tatiana lay on a cot in the corner of the room. Zanna and Nath reclined in the thrones, and he was napping with his head tilted to the side. Dalsay stood behind the pedestal and briefly looked up as they arrived, but Gossamer wasn't in the room.

"What's going on?" Tatiana sat up and rubbed her eyes. "Is the Apparatus of Ruune complete?"

"Not that I know of, but Black Frost is close. Slick and Slicer spotted him. He comes from the east and will be here by morning," Grey Cloak said.

"That's not possible. It should take him at least another day or half a day." Tatiana joined them in front of the mural. "Dalsay, use the mural. Look east."

Nath stretched out his arms, yawned, then smacked his lips. "What's the problem now?"

"We're about to get the kiss of death from Black Frost again," Zanna replied. "But this might be the last one."

Grey Cloak twisted around and said to his mother, "Is that a vote of confidence or the opposite?"

"It's either us or him." His mother joined him and held his face in both hands. "I'm proud of you. You've done everything you can. Don't doubt yourself now. Finish this."

"I plan to." He hugged his mother in a tight embrace. Then he took Zora by the hand. "We're going back to Dwarf Skull. Like it or not, Queen Rhonna, here I come."

31

Outside of the armory in Dwarf Skull, the face of every member of Talon fell when Grey Cloak broke the news about the coming of Black Frost.

Crane's mouth dropped open. Shannon reached over and lifted his chin until his mouth clacked shut.

"Lythlenion," Grey Cloak said. "You have to go inside. Tell Rhonna that Black Frost is on our doorstep, and as much confidence as I have in the dwarves, it will be impossible to stop him."

"They don't have to stop him—they need to slow him as long as they can." The burly orc's receding hair was full but white as a sheet, and his beard was neatly trimmed. A cleric warrior, he wore a dwarven-made breastplate that sculpted his well-knit frame. He put his hands on one of the barn doors. "As much as I desire to interfere, I cannot do it."

"Would it hurt to knock?" Grey Cloak asked.

Razor stood with a foot propped against the wall, his hands twisting the hilt of his sword. "Don't think we haven't knocked. We have. Well, I have."

Everyone looked pointedly at the blademaster.

"Well." Razor shrugged. "They need to get this done. I need to find Gorva."

Grey Cloak stepped back to the other side of the street, where he could see the chimney spewing out thick, black smoke. When he'd been young, he'd spent many days working in Rhonna's forge, pounding out horseshoes and farm blades. He knew what it took to make something out of metal. With dwarven expertise, he'd thought it would be easy. "They've been going at it day and night. There must be a hundred dwarves in there. Why isn't it done? Rhonna needs to know what is happening outside."

"Has Rhonna ever let us down before, brother?" Dyphestive put a hand on Grey Cloak's shoulder.

Grey Cloak eyed him. Dyphestive tended to get along with Rhonna better than he did. She was always walking down Grey Cloak's back. "We aren't on the farm anymore. This is the end of everything. We can't wait for everything to be perfect. It's now or never!" He crossed back over to the other side of the street and kicked the door. "Rhonna! We need the artifact, and we need it now. Black Frost is on the doorstep!"

Zora pulled his arm back. "That's not going to help."

Grey Cloak pressed his ear to the door. The distinct sound of metal striking metal worked in a steady cadence. The roar of furnace fires being stoked was constant. The dwarven smiths' efforts were in a hardworking, harmonious synchrony. Their creation would be a masterpiece once it was finished.

"They are still working at it as much as yesterday." Grey Cloak shook his head. "I don't know what to say, but I'm going back to the tower." He looked at the horizon. The stars were fading, and the darkness began to welcome the new day. "It's time for everyone to dragon up. The time to ride the sky has come."

TALON and the children of Cinder gathered on the vast top of the Wizard Watch. The lone remaining tower was the largest of them all, a stark obelisk casting a shadow over the white-brown land of Crow Valley.

To the north, as the top rim of the sun rose in the east, the Black Guard marched toward the tower. Fully armored with spear tips pointed skyward, they appeared as a sea of obsidian ants, growing in size with each step.

Riskers led the way, crossing back and forth in front of the army in a slow and lazy pattern of flight.

Back on the tower, Grey Cloak stood between the battlements and addressed the group. "The Riskers are our main concern. No doubt they will try to destroy the dwarven siege machines. It's up to us to prevent that."

Atop Cinder, who was centered among his children, Anya said, "If we take the initiative, we can prevent them from getting close."

Grey Cloak fought the urge to give her an irritated look. "That is why I am going to let you lead the assault while a handful of us will remain back, in case they slip through your defenses."

"They are middlings. We won't let them through our net," Anya said.

He nodded. "I'm going to hang back with Streak."

The dragon popped his head up. "Excuse me, what? I want to fight, not stand around and wait."

"We have to wait for the signal from Dwarf Skull when the Apparatus of Ruune is done." He looked east. "And keep an eye out for Black Frost."

Grey Cloak fully expected the monster dragon to appear at any moment, but the humongous overlord hadn't appeared yet. His chest tightened. The last thing he wanted to rely on was an artifact from another world, but they'd tried everything to stop Black Frost to no avail.

Dyphestive climbed inside the battlement beside his brother. "Don't despair, brother. There is always another way. We will find it."

"Yes, well, today is one of these days where I can't think of something. I can't believe that Rhonna is letting us down. We need that artifact." He shook his head. "The longer Black Frost lives, the more of us fall. I'm tired of seeing our comrades die." His jaw clenched. "This senseless bloodshed must come to an end."

"Just remember, he started it," Dyphestive reminded him. "We'll find a way to finish it."

"Grey Cloak, look!" Zora tugged on his cloak and turned him south. "Is that the signal?"

A bright star of light exploded in the far distance. He ran to the other side of the tower and jumped onto the wall. "That must be it!"

Dalsay floated up through the roof and confirmed the news. "Rhonna sends the signal. The Apparatus of Ruune is ready."

"Ah-ha!" Grey Cloak jumped down off the wall and grabbed the Stone of Transport. "I'll return to Dwarf Skull and bring it back here. Does anyone else want to see the unveiling?"

"Surprise us," Reginald the Razor said as he drew his sword. "I've got some fight I need to get out of me."

Anya nodded. "As do I."

Grey Cloak waved and vanished.

32

For the longest time, Grey Cloak stood with his mouth hanging open. He'd teleported himself outside of the armory doors and had met Lythlenion and Crane, who'd escorted him inside. The sweltering forge reeked of dwarf sweat, hot coals, and molten metal.

The dwarves stood along the center aisle, clawing their calloused hands through their beards and passing down large tankards brimming with ale. Not a one of them said a word to him, but they grunted and grumbled as Grey Cloak and his escort passed.

Queen Rhonna waited at the far end of the room, wearing a black leather apron and carrying a hammer in one hand. Her hair was tied up in a bun, and large drops of sweat beaded her face, which she wiped off with a red, checkered handkerchief.

"It's finished," she said.

Grey Cloak looked around. He'd seen a hand-drawn depiction of the Apparatus of Ruune, and there wasn't anything that resembled it in the room. He tilted his head over his shoulder. "Where is it?"

She pointed her stubby finger in the air.

Grey Cloak looked up to find the artifact. That was when his mouth dropped open.

Crane rubbed his own sagging jaw. "Magnificent. It's magnificent!"

Rhonna wiped her grubby hands on her handkerchief and proudly said, "Big, isn't it? We increased the dimensions to maximize firepower." She tapped one of the apparatus's four legs with her hammer. "Solid as a mountain of steel. You'll need to anchor it with spikes because I'm certain that it's going to kick. Never seen the likes of it. All of my kindred are giddy. They can't wait to see what it does. As a matter of fact…"

Rhonna's voice faded as Grey Cloak's thoughts were flooded in awe of the massive contraption. He ran his hand over the warm metal of the weapon's leg then walked under the base and touched another. He stepped out from underneath its shadow, hopped up on a table, and marveled at the rest of it. "It's as big as a dragon—a grand dragon."

Lythlenion moved to the front, reached up from his tiptoes, and touched the bottom of the weapon's barrel. He spun slowly underneath of it. "Is this cylinder where the weapon fires from?"

"Indeed." Rhonna beamed. "This contraption opened up an entire can of worms. We learned how to make new weapons from it."

At the back, the Apparatus of Ruune had a solid body bigger than a wagon. On the very top of the main chamber was an oversized spyglass with a scope that fed down the side. Under the eyepiece was a bench made out of solid metal perfectly contoured for sitting. The bench was large enough for a man, but undersized compared to the rest of the contraption. A small ladder led up to it. The weapon was more unique than anything he'd ever seen before. There were raised dwarven runes on the top of the chamber, strange wheels and gears, and other intricate mechanical shapes all over it.

"What are those?" He pointed at metal balls stacked up under the artifact. Each ball had arcane symbols carved in the dull brass and fluting that gave them a hollowed-out look.

Rhonna walked over to the pile and kicked them. "These giant pellets shoot right out of the barrel. The Thunderstones give them firepower. It will be glorious destruction when they hit their target."

"And where do we load the Thunderstones?" Grey Cloak asked.

Rhonna waved him over to another work table. A large metal egg with five chambers and a strange hose sticking out of the top sat upright on the table.

He jumped off the table and joined her.

"I take it this is the housing for the stones."

She nodded. "It will feed their energy through the tube into the chamber and charge the pellets. But the apparatus has more than one setting. It will fire the pellets, or it can be switched to pure energy. The concern there is that it might melt the barrel. The pellets will make it hot enough. It's a last resort."

Grey Cloak traced his finger over the iron surface and looked back over his shoulder at the apparatus. "Don't be offended, but how do we know it will work?"

A group of nearby Dwarves pounded their fists on their table, glared at Grey Cloak, and grunted.

He raised his hands. "Apologies. I know better." He looked down at Rhonna. "How do we get it out of here?"

"We'll take the legs off, load it into wagons, and haul it to Crow Valley."

"Rhonna, we can't wait that long. That will take the better part of a day. Black Frost and the Black Guard are almost on the tower's doorstep."

She scratched her head with the clawed tip of her hammer. "Well, you better think of something."

"Zooks, I was afraid you were going to say that."

ANYA, Dyphestive, Razor, and Shannon took to the sky with Streak and the other dragons. They left Zora behind with Fenora to wait for Grey Cloak.

Zora faced east with her hands between the battlements. Fenora was by her side like a loyal hound, her head resting between the structures.

"It's hard to imagine that this will all be over," Fenora said, "one way or the other. I want to have a perfect seat when we destroy Black Frost."

"You won't get a better view than this one." Zora looked behind her. "I wonder what is taking Grey Cloak so long. He should have reappeared by now."

Fenora stuck her head out over the edge to where she could see Zora. "Maybe he's getting something to eat. I'm sure he's hungry."

"No." Zora picked her lips. "He doesn't eat very much. Well, he didn't used to anyway."

"You are fond of him, aren't you?"

Zora didn't reply.

"He's very handsome by your standards. Charming, too, wouldn't you say?"

"Yes, that goes without saying." She stood up between the pyramid-capped battlements. "Shouldn't we be talking about something else at a time like this?" She spied the Black Guard's troops advancing at a trot. "The battle is about to begin."

"Sorry, but I enjoy the conversation. You know, a little girl talk never hurts." Fenora scratched one of her horns against the battlements. "We can go down there and get in on the action if you want?"

"No, we should wait." Zora squinted. In the far east, dark clouds were rolling in. "It looks like a storm coming, but I don't see lightning or rain."

Fenora stretched her neck out farther. "That's because that isn't a storm cloud you see."

"What is it?" Zora demanded.

Fenora rose and looked down at Zora. "That's Black Frost." She swung her steady gaze back toward the enemy. "Dragons, have mercy! He's huge!"

"What do we do?"

"Climb on. We need to tell the others."

Zora grabbed Fenora by the reins. "You go tell the others. I'll wait on Grey Cloak."

Fenora winked. "As you wish. Be sure to tell your boyfriend I said hello." She spread her wings and dropped off of the tower.

Zora watched her glide away. "Boyfriend? What does that even mean?"

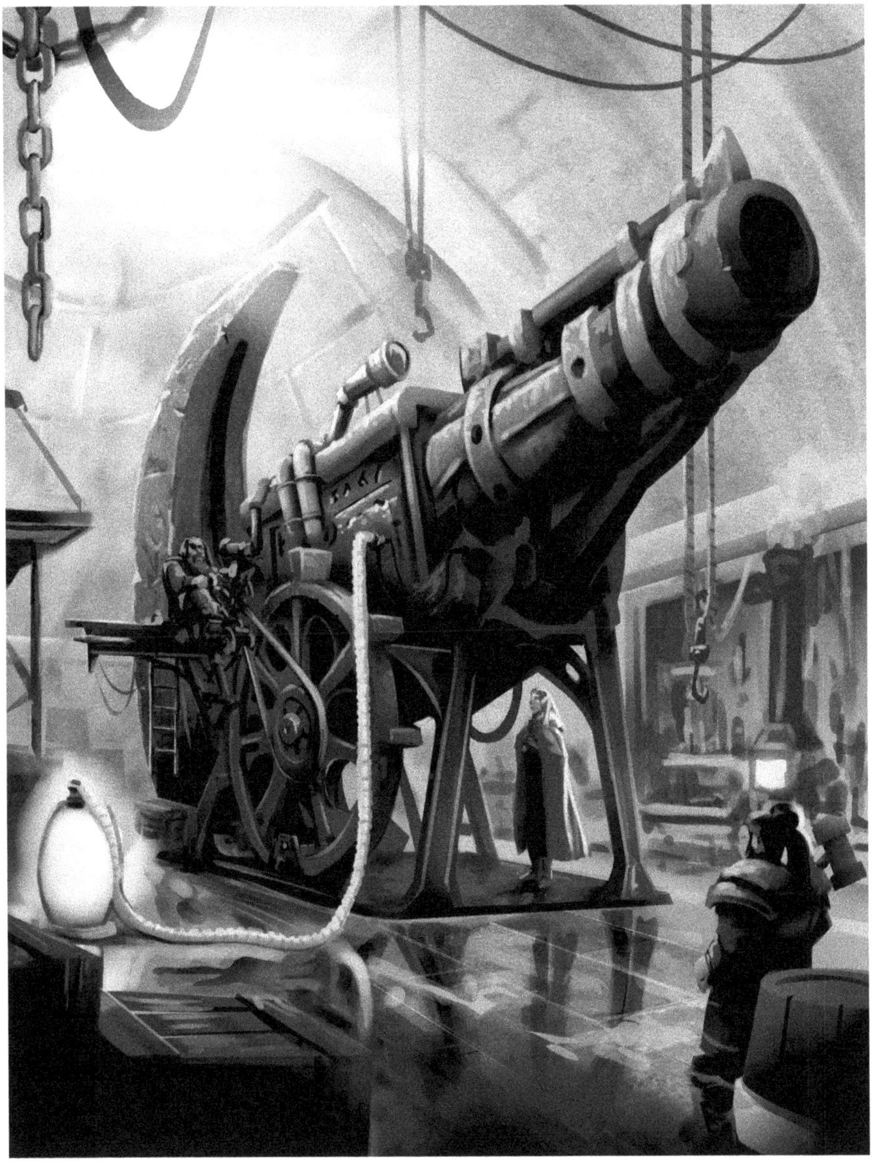

33

Grey Cloak appeared on the top of the Wizard Watch and found Zora sitting against the outer wall with her face buried in her hands.

He rushed to her side. "What's wrong? And where is everyone?"

"Where have you been?" She hopped to her feet and pulled him over to the wall. "That's what's wrong."

His blood chilled. "Black Frost. He's definitely closer than I'd hoped."

Zora looked him over. "Where's the weapon? Don't tell me it isn't finished?"

"No, it's completed, but there's a bit of a transportation problem."

She raised an eyebrow. "What do you mean?"

He spread out his arms. "It's huge. As big as Cinder. The

dwarves wanted to drive it here on wagons."

"On wagons? Are they fools? It's impossible for them to make it here in time." She pointed at Black Frost, who could be seen over a league in the distance. "He's right there!"

"Yes, I know." He sprang between the battlements and spied the Sky Riders approaching the Riskers. He looked back at Zora. "It's going to take four grands to carry the apparatus here. The dwarves are getting it ready for transport, but it won't be easy."

"Can't you use the Stone of Transport to bring it?"

"I tried, but I can only transport the living and certain belongings. I'm going to attempt to do what Dirklen did. Meanwhile, send word to Tatiana." He looked toward Black Frost. "Tell them they have to slow him down by any means possible. We need all the time we can get."

She nodded. "I'll do it." She reached up and squeezed his hand. "I know you can pull this off, but be careful."

"We'll see." He spotted Fenora in the distance, vanished, then reappeared in her saddle.

Fenora's head whipped around. "What the dragon? Where'd you come from?"

Raising his voice above the wind, he called, "The tower! Listen to me. We need to catch up with the other dragons. I'm going to transport four of you back to Dwarf Skull!"

"What for?"

"We have to transport the apparatus. It's solid metal and as big as you."

North of their position, he spotted the Sky Riders closing in on the Riskers. "Gooseberries. Listen, Fenora, I need you to veer back and wait for me at the tower. I'll send others back as well."

"You're the leader. Veering away."

As Fenora twisted around, Grey Cloak set his gaze on the riderless Streak. The Stone of Transport pulsed in his hand, and in the next instant, he sat on Streak's back. "Hello!"

Streak bucked in the air. "Will you stop doing that? You're scaring the dung out of everyone." He twisted his head around. "What's going on?"

"We have to catch up with Anya. Speed up."

"No problem." Streak's wings flapped faster. He jetted past the other dragons and got up to Cinder.

Grey Cloak flagged Anya down, which drew a scowl from the battle-hungry woman.

"What?" she shouted.

"Black Frost is here!" He pointed southeast. "I need two more grands! I'm taking them back to the tower to transport the apparatus!"

Anya shook her head. "What am I supposed to do, fight them all by myself?"

"Would you have it any other way?"

She cracked a smile.

"Listen, we need time. Buy all of it you can."

Anya gave him a knowing nod.

Cinder added, "Take Chubby and Bellarose. They aren't fastest in a fight, but they can carry a large load quicker than the rest. I'll send them back."

Grey Cloak saluted. "Ride the sky!"

Dyphestive and Rock caught up with them. "What is going on, brother Streak?"

"We're running out of time, that is what. Anya will fill you in. In the meantime, slow that army down."

"Will do!"

Grey Cloak placed his open hand on Streak's neck. "Are you ready to take the shortcut?"

The dragon's pink tongue flicked out of his mouth. "You know it. Let's go!"

"Here we go!"

In one wink of an eyelash, they were flying over Crow Valley. By the next, they glided above Dwarf Skull.

Streak landed in the streets in front of the armory. "Now what?"

He patted his dragon between the horns. "Wait right here. I'll be right back."

34

Zanna led Zora down the winding stone steps that spiraled through the heart of the Wizard Watch. "You look pale."

"I feel pale." Zora carried in her hand the small box that worked with the Medallion of Location. "On the tower top, I couldn't help but think I was witnessing the world coming to an end. The sight of Black Frost was horrifying, and I was all alone."

Zanna held her free hand. "Well, you aren't alone now."

"How can you remain calm at a time like this?"

"Panic won't serve me any better."

They exited the stairwell and entered the Time Mural chamber. Tatiana stood beside Gossamer, their attention fixed on the image of Black Frost hurtling toward them. Dalsay remained by the pedestal, and Nath sat quietly on the throne.

When Tatiana turned and saw Zora, she reached for her. "Dear sister, come!"

They hugged.

"It is good to be together again." Tatiana squeezed her tighter. "I know the timing is awful, but if I die, I will die fighting for my friends."

"I'm with you." Zora held out the jewel box. "I brought this." She flipped open the lid. The green dot in the black sand appeared. "Grey Cloak has not moved. But it has not been very long."

Zanna tapped her finger on the pommel of one of her swords. "He'll come through." She gazed at the picture.

The image in the archway panned back and forth between the Black Guard army coming from the north and Black Frost flying from the east. The Black Guard was closing in on the dwarven troops, who were the last barrier between Black Frost and the dragons.

Below the clouds, outnumbered Sky Riders battled Riskers in a furious fight for aerial supremacy. Flames and glowing energy projectiles lit up the morning sky.

"I should be out there." Zora's fingernails needled her elbows.

"I am sorry to mention it, but even with our forces, the attack of Black Frost is inevitable," Gossamer said. "Even with our defenses, there is nothing to stop him from landing right on top of us. He can fly over the dwarves and burn them to a crisp if he wishes."

Zora looked inside the box. Still no movement. She closed it.

Zanna took a step toward the mural. With her head tilted back, she pointed up. "What is that? Look."

An erratic, feathery flock of winged creatures approached Black Frost from the south.

"I'll move the image closer," Dalsay said.

Slowly, the mural magnified the image of the strange flying mass in the sky. A closer look revealed hundreds, if not thousands, of gnomes riding on the backs of giant vultures.

Zora's heart leaped inside her chest. "It's the Southern Storm!"

"Who?" Gossamer asked.

"They are led by Jumax, a natural," she said. "If anyone can slow down Black Frost, he can."

Leading from the front, Gorva flew on a giant vulture alongside Jumax, who rode on one as well.

He greeted her with a big, bright smile. "Gorva, Princess, Beautiful One, I never imagined a vision as spectacular as you, but I believe this Black Frost tops all. He is a mountain of a monster. It will be a joy to take him down."

"I'm glad you think so!"

"Durmost!" he hollered over his shoulder where the dwarven commander's vulture flew.

The gnome rose in the saddle, waiting for Jumax's orders.

"We will be wise about this. Attack in waves. All of our efforts will be focused on the left wing. Surely, he cannot fly with only one. I'll lead the way. Catch his attention and let our wicked enemy come face-to-face with those who will take him down."

"Aye!" Durmost saluted.

Gorva hoisted up onto her shoulder the spear that Jumax had provided her. "I hope you don't plan to introduce yourself without me?"

"Never, my princess!" With his feathers rustling in the wind, he eyed Black Frost. "Ugh! Look at him. Part of his face is missing."

Gorva noticed exposed muscle underneath Black Frost's damaged scales. A large part of his eye was bloodshot. "He can be hurt. He's not invincible!"

"Nothing is when I'm around!" The sleek and muscular bare-chested warrior balanced on his saddle as they flew above Black Frost. "We might be as canaries on a horse's back, but he is one! We are many!" He dove from the vulture's back and soared toward Black Frost.

If the gargantuan dragon noticed them, he didn't show it. Black Frost remained on a straight path toward the Wizard Watch.

Gorva dug her heels into her vulture's ribs. It let out an ugly squawk and sped after Jumax. She caught up with him as Jumax landed between the dragon's towering horns, which were the size of trees. She jumped out of the big bird's saddle, tumbled in the air, then landed like a cat beside Jumax on Black Frost's head.

He looked into the distance. "An interesting view. I feel as if I'm flying on a hunk of land." He drew his sword then extended his free hand to her. "Come. It is time that we properly introduce ourselves."

Together, they descended the bridge of scales that ran down between the dragon's horns to his snout. They stopped to face Black Frost's eyes, which were several yards away.

"I am Jumax!" he proudly stated.

Black Frost's eyes focused on both of them.

"Wicked one!" Jumax continued. "Today, you meet your conquerors! Enjoy your last breath, and prepare to die!"

A shock passed through their bodies, ruffling Jumax's feathers and knocking the two of them off balance. At the same time, the first wave of the Southern Storm that had attached themselves to the dragon's wing blew up in a cloud of smoke and feathers. Their lifeless bodies crashed toward the earth.

Pain soaked Gorva's skin all the way to the bone. She lost her grip on Jumax's hand and all control of her body. She fell off one side of Black Frost's snout, and he fell from the other.

35

Grey Cloak stood inside of the Dwarf Skull's northern gate. He waved his arm in a huge circle. "Rhonna! Can't you get those wagons moving faster? There's a war going on."

The dwarven queen stood on the wagon that was towing the main body of the Apparatus of Ruune. "Watch your tone, or one of my soldiers is liable to cut it off!" she fired back as she passed him. Then she shouted to the front: "Dwarves, put your backs into it, or we'll miss the war! And we don't want that, do we?"

The dwarves replied as one. "We want war! We want more! We want war!"

Forty stout men, split into two groups, towed the apparatus using heavy ropes. It took them over an hour to load the massive metal contraption, which was broken into several parts. The legs were detached, and they'd have to assemble it again at the tower.

Streak, Fenora, Chubby, and Bellarose waited outside of the

gate, sitting like dogs. Streak and Fenora had bored looks on their faces, and Chubby yawned. Bellarose followed his example.

The wagon inched along at an agonizing pace and hadn't yet made it halfway through the main gate. Grey Cloak ran his hand over his face, leaned against the open gate, and sighed.

"I heard that," Rhonna grumbled. "If you like, you could pull it yerself."

"No thanks, but I wish I'd brought Dyphestive."

Streak scratched behind his earhole with his back leg then flopped his paw back on the ground.

"This is ridiculous." Fenora marched over to the dwarves. "No offense, but why don't you handsome bearded fellas let a lady handle this?"

Every dwarf looked over their shoulder at Rhonna.

She gave them an approving nod.

They dropped the rope.

"Good thinking, Fenora," Streak said.

"I know." Fenora took both ropes in her mouth and pulled the cords over her shoulders. She leaned forward, clawed feet digging into the dirt, and started taking one step at a time.

"Go, Fenora!" Grey Cloak pushed off the wall. He caught Rhonna shaking her head as she passed by. "What?"

"If you're in such a hurry, why didn't you think of that earlier?"

"Why didn't you think of it?" he replied.

"Because I'm not a Sky Rider." Rhonna's cheeks fattened up when she smiled. She rolled by with the wind in her face.

Grey Cloak walked at a brisk pace beside the wagon. The tension in his shoulders started to ease as Fenora towed the apparatus into the wide open, giving the dragons room to take flight.

Fenora stopped and looked back at him. "I might have made it look easy, but this contraption is heavier than it looks."

"We can handle it," Chubby said in a slow and deep voice. "Hook us up, little beards."

"You heard 'em, dwarves!" Rhonna said as she lifted her hammer off of her shoulder and waved it over her head. "Hitch those dragons to the chains."

The apparatus had four giant eyelets welded onto the outside of the main frame. Each chain had a hook on the end.

Streak, Fenora, Chubby, and Bellarose moved to the corners of the wagon. The dwarves attached the chains to their harnesses.

Rhonna jumped from the wagon and approached Grey Cloak. "We're going to have to go with you to set up the artifact."

"I wouldn't have it any other way." He extended his arm. "Pick a dragon. I don't think any of them have been ridden by a queen before." He started to pat the bun on her head then withdrew when one of the dwarven soldiers moved in with his battle-ax.

Rhonna raised four stubby fingers. The dwarves from their earlier escape came forward. The blond and raven-haired dwarves climbed onto Chubby in the back. And the chestnut-haired and redhead saddled up on Bellarose.

"I'll ride Fenora." Rhonna walked to where Fenora and Streak were positioned on the front. "She has grit."

Grey Cloak climbed into Streak's saddle and stood up in his stirrups. "Everyone, grab a leg!"

The dragons exchanged confused looks as their heads twisted toward one another.

"The legs of the apparatus." Grey Cloak pointed at the four disassembled pieces resting on the side of the wagon. "Help yourselves, but don't eat them. They don't taste like cattle."

Each dragon grabbed a leg in their mouths and faced forward.

Rhonna held the reins in a white-knuckled grip.

Fenora looked up at her. "It will be fine. Haven't you flown before?"

"No, and I wouldn't, either, but I wouldn't make my dwarves do something I wouldn't do myself."

"Streak. Fenora. Lead the way!" Grey Cloak said.

All four dragons moved as one, towing the contraption on the wagon and rumbling down the road that led to Dwarf Skull. They picked up speed while keeping their wings folded behind their backs.

Behind them, the dwarves let out wild cheers and waved them on. Many of them ran alongside the wagon, short legs pumping as fast as they could until they couldn't keep up anymore.

Grey Cloak shouted at Fenora as they continued to gain speed. "Are you ready?

With her mouth full of the metal leg, she nodded.

He patted Streak on the horns. "On your lead!"

Streak spread out his wings. Fenora followed suit along with Chubby and Bellarose.

The dragons went into one last final sprint and jumped. The Apparatus of Ruune lifted off from the wagon. The dragons rose and dipped down suddenly, then the artifact dragged across the road, tearing the pavement up.

"Come on, dragons! You can do it!" Grey Cloak watched the apparatus skid across the ground. It skipped one more time off the road, then the dragons lifted it into the sky and soared toward the clouds.

Grey Cloak looked over at Rhonna. Her eyes were as big as the moon, and she was as pale as a bedsheet. He waved.

She let out a breath and nodded.

"I don't mean to sound pushy," he said as he leaned toward Streak's earhole. "But we need to get there as fast as we can."

Streak nodded and mumbled with a mouthful of metal, "Will do, boss. Will do."

36

"Nooo!" Zora clutched her cheeks as she watched Gorva plummet toward the ground from over a thousand feet in the air. "Someone, do something!"

Grey Cloak appeared out of thin air beside Zora. "I hope I didn't startle you this time. What's our situation?"

Zora looked between him and the mural. "You!" She pointed at Gorva, who careened to her death. She grabbed his face and said, "Save her!"

"On it!"

Grey Cloak popped out of view and reappeared in midair beside Gorva. As gravity pulled them down, he wrapped one arm around her waist and smirked. "Miss me?"

"No comment," she replied.

The Cloak of Legends billowed out, and they made a slow descent toward the dusty terrain.

"Look up!" called a voice from above. Jumax swooped in and caught them both up in his massive arms. "Ingenious. The little elf man can float."

"It's not me—it's the cloak."

Jumax's brow raised. "Interesting."

The trio touched down.

"What happened?" Grey Cloak asked.

Gorva broke out of Jumax's grasp. "Black Frost sent a jolt through us that could fry cattle."

"Curious that Black Frost didn't use that on Dyphestive and me. Perhaps it was because he was covered by his own people."

A rainfall of the dead, giant vultures and sky gnomes, crashed into the land surrounding them.

"My kindred!" Jumax roared. He let out a shrieking cry.

Two giant vultures landed beside him. "Gorva, come! We will avenge our brood!"

"Our brood?" Grey Cloak asked.

She gave him a snarl and walked away.

"Gorva," he said catching up to her and Jumax. "What are you going to do? Attack him the same way?"

She jumped into the vulture's saddle. "We have to slow him down somehow."

Jumax glared at Black Frost. "We will shred those wings through the membranes. Pierce them. Gore them! Jumax has a plan!" He and Gorva's vultures took flight.

"Zooks, it wouldn't be a bad idea if Black Frost couldn't shock them to death." Grey Cloak had a thought. "Hmm, no reason I can't help." He looked down at the Stone of Transport in his grip and squeezed.

He appeared on Black Frost's back, brought around the Rod of Weapons, and summoned a large-headed blade like a halberd. He launched himself up at Black Frost's tremendous wing, slashed a hole clean through, and jumped through the space to land on the other side. "Huh. One cut, only a thousand more to go."

A wave of vultures by the scores flew at Black Frost and started landing on his left wing. The gnomes, armed with short blades, jumped onto the membrane. The vultures clawed at the thick flesh with their beaks. Grey Cloak sliced an entire man-sized section out of the wing.

Led by Jumax and Gorva, more members of the Southern Storms army started to land on the dragon's back and wing.

The Cloak of Legends pulsed.

Grey Cloak waved frantically at Gorva and Jumax. "Get away! Get away!" He leaped off the dragon.

The vultures and gnomes scattered away from Black Frost as a charge of energy rippled underneath his scales.

Once it passed, Grey Cloak landed and waved them back. "Attack! Attack!" He shouted at Gorva. "I can feel it before it comes! Follow my signal!"

Gorva nodded and spoke to Jumax.

In the waning seconds between Black Frost's defenses, more vultures flocked on his wings from the tip to the bottom in a pecking frenzy. Holes in the ginormous dragon's wings started to spread and rip.

Once again, the Cloak of Legends pulsed.

Grey Cloak signaled them again. "Move!"

Vultures and gnomes scattered like pigeons. Grey Cloak felt the energy flow underneath of his jump and watched the scales ripple. As he landed, he plunged the Rod of Weapons into another patch of flesh and sliced it open.

In tens, twenties, then hundreds, the vultures landed on the wing and tore the flesh away like hungry scavengers.

Black Frost wobbled in the air. His left wing flapped vigorously, shaking off vultures and gnomes, only to have them land back on the same spot.

The left wing had more gaping holes in it than skin. The vultures chewed up the carpet of flesh and dropped through the holes to attack another area.

The cloak sent Grey Cloak another warning. He waved his arms and jumped. Vultures and their riders scattered. All of a sudden, Black Frost barrel-rolled in the sky, shaking more of the pesky enemy off.

Grey Cloak didn't see the energy rippling through the dragon's scales until it was too late. The Southern Storm started to land.

"No!" he shouted as he floated in the air. "Not yet!"

A jolt of energy fired through Black Frost's body, taking hundreds of vultures and gnomes down. Plumes of feathers went up like chimney smoke. Flesh burned to a crisp. Dead birds and fried gnomes rained down from the sky.

But that time, Black Frost went with them. In a slow circle, he glided helplessly toward the ground. His shredded wing had been made useless. The claws on his back feet flexed out. He prepared for a crash landing.

From the monster's back, Grey Cloak met Gorva and Jumax's eyes. All of them threw their arms up and cheered. "We did it!"

Black Frost crashed feet first on the ground. His momentum caused his head to whip down, and the great overlord ate a mouthful of dirt. He pushed up from the suffocating dust, roared with a thousand dragon voices as one, and started to slink toward the tower with murder in his blazing blue eyes.

37

Anya grabbed a bow and a handful of arrows from a quiver that bounced along Cinder's saddle. She placed two arrows in her mouth and nocked the third on the bowstring. "Not my favorite choice of weapon, but it will have to do."

"What's that?" Cinder asked.

"Nothing." She fed her wizard fire into the loaded arrow and the ones in her mouth at the same time. The tips turned as white-hot as a sun. "Catch up with the winged lizard and the fiend on his back. I have a delivery for them."

Cinder flapped his wings faster. "Aye, aye."

The Sky Riders were outnumbered by the Riskers more than two to one. Ten Riskers were on a path to attack the dwarves and their siege machines. The other members chased the Sky Riders and attacked from behind.

An arrow whizzed by Anya's head and clacked off of Cinder's horn. She twisted around in her saddle.

A female orc Risker bore down on Cinder, riding the wind on a middling dragon. They closed in while she loaded another arrow.

"Fool!" Anya turned around and fired back. Her arrow streaked toward the enemy and punched a hole in the Risker's breastplate.

The orc's eyes popped open as she grabbed the arrow and tried to pull it out. When she died and fell out of the saddle, her dragon veered away.

"What happened? Did you kill one?" Cinder asked.

"Of course." In the blink of an eye, Anya loaded another arrow, stood up in her stirrups, and aimed at a Risker on a grand in front of her. The rider sat tall in the saddle and had a broad back. He looked over his shoulder in time to see the arrow blast a hole in his back and stick out through his chest. He slumped forward but did not fall.

"That puts the odds back in our favor."

Two Riskers raced above then dove at them. They rode on middling dragons and were too fast for Cinder to catch.

Slick chased after the Riskers. Razor and Slicer brought up the rear then shot past him. They caught up with the Riskers, and Slicer ripped one man from his saddle with his back talons.

The Risker had drawn a sword but was dropped a moment before he swung. Razor pumped his sword in the air and saluted back to Anya.

Slick closed in on the final Risker but didn't catch up until it breathed flame on one of the dwarves' assault towers and set it ablaze. With Slick on his tail, the enemy dragon skimmed over the dwarven ranks and added more fuel to the fire. The bearded warriors were smothered in dragon flame.

A volley of fire from dwarven crossbows came and punched a score of holes into the enemy. Feathered with crossbow bolts, the middling dragon prepared for another flaming pass. Horns first, Slick hit the dragon head-to-head and drove it down from the sky. The moment it collided with the ground, dwarves with heavy axes swarmed it like ants and chopped both Risker and dragon down into the dirt.

DYPHESTIVE'S AIM was about as good with a javelin as it was with a bow and arrow—horrible. He slung another javelin at a Risker flying behind him and missed their dragon's wing by the better part of a foot. He had aimed for the Risker. "Anvils! I'm atrocious at this!"

"Have you hit anything yet?" Rock asked.

"Does the sky count?"

Rock grumbled. "Give me a javelin. Perhaps I can throw one better!"

Dyphestive hunkered down behind his buckler and blocked another arrow. Two were already stuck in the shield. He looked across the sky and spotted Shannon riding Feather. They had a Risker on the run while another chased them.

Shannon stretched the bowstring along her cheek and let the missile fly. It struck the Risker in the back shoulder.

Using her wings, Feather thrust herself into a loop and barrel-rolled at the same time. They twisted above their pursuers then dropped in right behind them.

With another arrow nocked, Shannon fired then nailed the second Risker square in the back.

"She's great!" Dyphestive smiled broadly. "A natural! Together, they are in perfect harmony!"

Aided by the mystic harnesses, the dragons' speed made up for what the Sky Riders lacked in numbers. The Riskers were being whittled down by superior skill and fighting spirit. But not all celebrated.

"I didn't join this fight to chase a dragon's tail. I want to kill something!" Rock said in a gusty, battle-ready voice. They were hunting one of the last Risker's grands. "And I can't catch this one even with the harness!"

Aside from Chubby and Bellarose, Rock was one of the slowest of Cinder's children, including Snags and Smash, who were in the thick of aerial battles of their own.

"You're blaming my extra weight, aren't you?" Dyphestive said.

"No, but you aren't nearly as light as the other riders. Hold on—he's diving!"

The Risker ahead of them swept over the dwarven ranks, washing them in dragon flame by the dozens then flying straight through an assault tower, busting it to pieces.

Something in Dyphestive's gut told him he was holding Rock

back. He started stripping gear off the dragon and lightening the load.

"What are you doing?"

"You need more speed. You're going to have it, but first, I want you to slow down and let our pursuers catch up!" He blocked another arrow with his shield.

"Why?"

"Trust me, I have a plan!"

Rock nodded and slowed.

The dragon behind them, a middling, caught up and nipped at Rock's tail.

Dyphestive stood up in the saddle, faced the enemy, and lifted the Iron Sword. He leaped, screaming, "It's thunder time!"

38

Dyphestive's blade connected in a clean cut to the neck, severing the middling dragon's head. Its body barrel-rolled out of control as Dyphestive crashed toward the rugged terrain less than a hundred feet below. He landed flat on his back, crushing small sandstones into dust with a resounding *thump*.

From inside the impression he'd made in the ground, Dyphestive sat up. Above, Rock caught up with the Risker and chomped down on the grand dragon's tail. They hit the ground at the same time, plowing through dwarven ranks before coming to a stop.

The Risker scrambled away from the two dragons and filled his hands with steel. A host of dwarves came at him with long spears and stuck him like a pig from multiple directions.

Scales and dragon flesh went flying as the two grand dragons clashed in a battle of might and muscle. Horns rammed together, locked up, and twisted back and forth. Smoky breath and snorts of fire spewed from the snarling beasts.

Rock broke away and released his full breath. The enemy grand matched flame for flame. They marched toward one another.

Dyphestive crawled out of the giant divot he'd made in the ground and found his sword lying nearby. He grabbed it.

The dragon breath attacks came to a stop. Each dragon charged, and the great lizards locked up in a knot of raw muscle. They rolled across the ground and crushed anything living or dead underneath their mass. Dwarves scattered, reformed their ranks, and shot crossbows or cast spears. They hit both dragons.

"No!" Dyphestive charged into the fray. "You're hitting the wrong dragon!" Between the dragons being entwined together into balls and their similar scale patterns, even he had trouble separating which was which. He called out. "Rock, which are you?"

"Stay out of it!" Rock said.

A tail with dark rings curled up from behind one of the dragons. The prehensile end grabbed the other dragon by the horn and yanked its head back. Jaws opened, and the winning dragon's teeth sank into the flesh of the exposed neck. An entire chunk of muscle was ripped out, leaving a nasty gaping wound. The dragon fell over dead on the ground. Its wings gave a final twitch, then it moved no more.

The dwarves surrounded the victorious dragon, their hardened steel bared.

Dyphestive watched the dragon spit out a bloody chunk of

flesh he'd had in his mouth. There were deep wounds all over his body, and blood splattered his scales. Dyphestive held up his arm to stop the advancing dwarves. "Rock?"

"You speak as if you doubt I was victorious. Of course it's me." Rock cast his gaze over his fallen foe. "He was a seasoned grand of many battles. He died with honor."

Dyphestive climbed on his dragon's back. "I hope you saved your strength because the fight is not over yet."

Rock shook his neck and spread his wings. "I'm barely winded. Let's ride the sky and bring down death on our enemies." With a booming roar, he launched himself into the sky and took flight.

On the surface, the dwarves hurried toward the battlefront in organized formations. Black Frost lay ahead, struggling as the army of dwarves tried to keep him down.

Grey Cloak watched in disbelief. Using chains and ropes, the dwarves swarmed Black Frost in an attempt to tether him to the ground.

Two teams lassoed the dragon's snout and tied it shut. Others fired giant harpoons that embedded themselves between the seams of Black Frost's scales. Chains were anchored into the rocky ground, constraining the dragon's front and back talons.

"I can't believe what I am seeing," he said to Jumax and Gorva, who stood by, observing with him.

Gorva leaned on her spear. "They are brilliant engineers.

Unlike you, they came with a plan in mind long before they arrived."

"Ha ha."

The longer they watched, the more tethers the dwarves attached. Black Frost struggled in the restraints, but that only made it worse for him. The dwarves used gears and levers mounted into the rock and cranked the notches tighter, spreading Black Frost's limbs back farther.

Thirty-foot-high assault towers fired more harpoons from the ballistae. Some connected then sank into the dragon's flesh.

Durmost the sky gnome landed near Jumax.

"What is it, brother?" Jumax asked.

The sky gnome's long nose crinkled, and his bulging eyes twitched. "Great One, Everything Magnificent, the Black Guard army advances on the dwarves' doorstep. They will sweep through the camp with superior numbers and free Black Frost."

"Summon our brethren. I'm certain the dwarves have weapons that we can drop on them from the sky." Jumax beat his chest. "The Southern Storm attacks! Gorva, join me!"

She looked at Grey Cloak.

He nodded. "If I see Razor, I'll say hello for you."

She poked a sword at him. "You'll say nothing or never speak again at all."

Grey Cloak held up the Stone of Transport, waved his fingers, and disappeared. He popped back inside the Wizard Watch. Everyone was still standing where he'd left them.

Dalsay had a clear view of the battlefield pulled up on the mural. All of the dwarves, over three thousand strong, dedicated themselves to holding down Black Frost. To the north, the Black Guard came at them in a dark wave of steel. There were no dwarven defenses to stop them.

"What do we do?" Zora asked as she bit her nails. "There aren't enough Sky Riders and vultures to stop them." She looked at Grey Cloak. "Where is the apparatus? We need it now."

"I know that. Trust me. It's coming." Grey Cloak stifled a doubtful look. *But I don't know whether it will be here soon enough.*

39

THE BATTLE IN THE SKIES WAS OVER. THE SKY RIDERS HAD WON out over the Riskers, but the ten-thousand strong Black Guard remained.

Grey Cloak appeared on the saddle with Dyphestive and Rock. "Tell Anya that we need to slow down that army the best that we can. I'll contact some of the others."

"Will do, brother."

Using the stone, he jumped from Rock's saddle and appeared on the back of Snags, who flew with Smash. He climbed between the dragon's horns and pointed at the troops below. "See them?"

Snags nodded.

"Make them taste fire!"

"I'd be happy to," the dragon answered in a gravelly voice. He dove with his brother.

The Sky Riders split into two separate groups. Each started on the opposite side of the army's ranks, flew over the soldiers' heads, and blasted them with flames.

Clothing and hair caught fire below. Many cooked inside their suits of metal plate and mail armor. The dragons wiped out the Black Guard by the scores, but some slipped through the flames. They marched on, evading that storm and advancing toward the exposed dwarves.

"Zooks! There are too many!"

Black Guard archers in the middle ranks came to a stop, loaded their bows, then unleashed a volley of arrows that blackened the sky.

Grey Cloak covered up on Snags's back. The missiles peppered the Sky Riders, ricocheting off of armor and scales but penetrating the membranes of the wings and weak spots in the armor.

He spotted Dyphestive as they passed by. His brother had three arrows stuck in his back and shoulders.

Below, the archers advanced and prepared another volley. The dragons could go after the archers, a soft spot in the ranks, but that would set the front ranks free to charge.

"There's no good way out of this!" he called to Snags.

Snags snorted flames. "They can't harm us with those little sticks. Let them try!"

Another volley rocketed into the air. At the same time, the dragons unleashed their flames without fear.

Black Guard soldiers by the hundreds pressed past the

smoke and flame. Growing in numbers, they moved through the obstacles like a dam that couldn't hold water.

"This is grim," Grey Cloak passed by Razor, who traveled the opposite way. He waved then pointed slightly north but mostly east.

A huge cloud of dust like a sand storm appeared behind the rocky dunes of the near horizon. A thunder of hooves caught his ear. He stood up in the stirrups. "What is that?"

Razor was shouting and waving his arms wildly, but he couldn't read his lips. It didn't look good.

"Great! Just what we need. More trouble!"

ZORA BREATHLESSLY WATCHED the valiant fight from all angles thanks to Dalsay's control. The dwarves had Black Frost caught in a web, but in her gut, she knew it wouldn't last for long. The Sky Riders sprayed fire at the ground, burning the enemy troops to a crisp, but there were far too many. Her shoulders sagged, and her chin sank to her chest.

Here I am, just standing here, doing nothing.

Strong hands landed on her shoulders and started to massage them. She smelled the faint scent of Tatiana's sweet perfume.

"Don't despair. It's not over yet." Tatiana's voice strengthened her. "Look."

From the northeast, a huge dust cloud rose from the ground.

Zora rose. "What's that?" She squinted as figures underneath the cloud started to take form. "Who is that?"

"An old friend of yours," Tatiana whispered in her ear, "and many friends of his."

"Dalsay, a closer look?" Zora asked. She tingled from head to toe.

The image in the mural shifted directions and moved in toward the new figures.

Riders on horseback numbering in the thousands lined up on the rise and lowered their lances. They wore light armor and acorn-shaped helmets and sat straight up with steely determination in their eyes. Zora knew who it was at once. *Elves!*

At the forefront was their leader, his bare-chested, well-defined frame and long jet-black hair unmistakable.

Zora gasped. "Bowbreaker!" Her heart danced. "How is this possible? How did they know?"

Zanna stepped forward. "Anything is possible when you control the Time Mural. Tatiana sent me back in time while you and Grey Cloak were gone. I visited Bowbreaker, pleaded my case, and hoped he would come."

In wedge formations, an elven cavalry led by Bowbreaker thundered down the rise into the terror-stricken Black Guard. The clamor of armored soldiers being run over by Bowbreaker's thousands could be heard through the tower's thick walls. Lancers picked off soldiers one and two at a time. The front ranks of the Black Guard and archers in the middle were decimated.

The fresh blood of enemies seeped into the sand. Hardened

soldiers' spirits were broken, their bodies crushed and bones turned to dust. The Black Guard invasion became a field of slaughter, and the panicked soldiers fought for their lives.

Amid the throng of battling bodies, Bowbreaker rode on a white-spotted stallion that was bigger than all of the others. The elf fed his bow from the twin quivers loaded across his back. At point-blank range, he feathered every soldier who attacked.

The bodies piled up. The dead did not rise. The mission of the Black Guard was over.

"Th-that was amazing." Zora held her hand over her thumping heart as she studied the blood-splattered figure of Bowbreaker. "We *won*."

Zanna stepped in front of Zora's awestruck gaze and turned her face toward the image of Black Frost. "It's not over until he is dead."

Black Frost's bonds started to break. His mighty roar shook the tower to its core. The floor trembled. The ground quaked.

Zora forgot all about Bowbreaker. "Rogues of Rodden! Nothing can stop him."

40

Zora met up with Grey Cloak, Dyphestive, and more members of Talon on the top of Wizard Watch. The three of them were looking south.

"They should be close," Grey Cloak said of Streak and the other dragons.

Razor and Shannon shared a spot between the battlements and hollered to them. "Grey Cloak! That big lizard is pulling free! If something doesn't happen, our biscuits are going to be burnt!"

Grey Cloak ran over to the east side with Zora gripping his hand. Razor was right. Black Frost pulled a rear leg free, and the dwarves' chains and ropes began to snap.

"To be honest, I'm surprised they kept him down this long." The trapped dragon stood no more than a few hundred yards away. "We have to keep fighting."

"But how?" Zora asked.

Dyphestive made a sharp whistle. Everyone turned in his direction. He pointed toward the southern hemisphere. "Look! Is that them?"

Grey Cloak practically jumped out of his boots. He ran over to join his brother. Sure enough, five black dots appeared in the sky. Four dragons carried a heavy metal contraption.

He chopped his arms back and forth. "Clear the center, everyone. Clear the center! They're coming!"

Zanna, Nath, and Tatiana emerged through the open hatch of the tower's stairwell.

"I see you saw them." Tatiana gazed skyward. "We came to tell you."

"They better get here fast!" Razor said. "Black Frost is busting loose!"

Several members of Talon were waving their arms at the dragons coming their way. "Hurry! Hurry!"

It felt like an eternity watching Streak and Fenora drag the apparatus through the sky. "They must be exhausted hauling that thing."

"Oh no!" Zora jerked Grey Cloak by the arm. "Look!"

A trio of Riskers that Grey Cloak hadn't seen before was on a collision course with the dragons carrying the artifact.

"Zooks! Tatiana, do you have the Star of Light?"

"Of course."

He fastened his hand on her wrist. "Hang on. You are coming with me."

All at once, they vanished and reappeared on Streak's back.

"Whoa! Who is that?" Streak asked out of the corner of his mouth. He managed a backward look. "Oh, it's you guys. Hello, Tatiana. You're looking as fine as ever."

Grey Cloak flagged down Rhonna and pointed northeast. "You have company!"

It didn't take the dwarves long to fill their hands with javelins from the oversized quivers on their dragons.

Riskers started firing arrows with sharp heads that were bright spots of energy.

Tatiana held out the Star of Light, creating a shield wall between them and the enemy.

Arrows skipped off the shimmering surface.

"I'll make this quick." In his hand, Grey Cloak's Rod of Weapons blossomed into a sharp-tipped spear. He took a breath through his nose and ignited the power of the Stone of Transport.

Even with the instantaneous teleportation, his mind rifled through a dozen thoughts, primarily of taking down his enemies. It was no time to show mercy. This was war. What had to be done wouldn't change.

He appeared behind a lead Risker, and before the man even knew he was there, Grey Cloak stabbed him in the heart.

The Riskers flying beside their leader took notice, and with their bows ready, they took aim and fired. Grey Cloak vanished as the arrows whizzed through the spot where his body had been. Their missiles sailed past, and the streaks of light nailed each Risker dead in the chest. All three men fell from the saddle, and their dragons veered away.

Grey Cloak reappeared on Streak's back seconds later.

"That was fast," Streak said. "Not as fast as me but fast."

"Impressive," Tatiana said as she tucked the Star of Light in her clothing.

The dragons closed in on the tower. From Grey Cloak's angle, he could see Black Frost starting to rise. His front paw swept through the army of dwarves. He scooped them up and crushed them to death.

"Ew!" Streak said. "He pulverized a handful of the bearded chipmunks."

"Faster, Streak! Faster, Fenora!" Grey Cloak said. "The apparatus is our only chance!"

The quartet of dragons made it to the Wizard Watch before Black Frost busted free of his final bonds. Rock, Smash, Snags, and Dyphestive waited on the rooftop, positioning themselves below the dragons.

As the dragons hovered above the tower, Grey Cloak hollered down to his companions, "Catch!"

Following Streak, Fenora, Chubby, and Bellarose dropped the legs of the Apparatus of Ruune. The three dragons waiting below caught them in their jaws, and Dyphestive caught the fourth oversized heavy object in his arms without so much as a grunt. He propped the leg up, and the dragons followed suit. All four legs touched at the top, forming a base.

Grey Cloak jumped off of Streak, landed in the middle of the legs, and guided the dragons down using his arms. "Easy, to the left. Now right. Forward. That's it, that's it. Right there."

The Apparatus of Ruune made a soft landing on its legs. The

dragons touched down on the tower. Rhonna and the four dwarves climbed down from their saddles then burst into action. Using heavy wrenches to thread nuts and bolts bigger than a man's head, they secured the apparatus to the base.

"Here!" Rhonna gave Dyphestive a sledgehammer from a tool sack and a handful of spikes as long as a man's arm. "Nail those legs down to the roof. If you don't, this thing will kick right off the rooftop. That won't do us a bit of good!"

Grey Cloak caught Zora marveling at the tremendous apparatus. "Bigger than you expected?"

"I never imagined," she mumbled.

"Nor did I." He hurried over to the wall.

Black Frost was peeling off the last of his bounds, and fire was in his eyes. "Anvils, we need a little more time. Streak!" He turned and found his dragon nose to nose with him.

"Right here, boss."

"I hate to ask, and I know it's risky, but the dragons need to distract him while we get this ready."

Streak nodded. "Don't worry. I know what to do, but we'll need all the help we can get."

"You'll have it. I'll signal Gorva and the Southern Storm. They'll follow your lead."

Streak hopped up onto the battlements. "Brothers and sisters, come with me. We have work to do!"

Grey Cloak reached up and petted Streak on his snout. "Be careful, brother."

Streak licked his hand. "Don't worry. I will."

All as one unit, the children of Cinder lifted off and joined their brethren in the sky.

41

Led by Streak, Anya, and Jumax, the dragons and vultures swarmed around Black Frost's face. They spat fire, scorching Black Frost's head around the eyes, darting in and out as he swiped at them.

His advance continued one ground-shaking step at a time. Vultures swarmed his eyes.

He scraped them away, but they formed a moving cloud over his head.

"Rhonna, you have to hurry!" Grey Cloak said as he watched on in horror. "They aren't slowing his trek!"

Dyphestive and the dwarves drove in the last of the spikes, securing the apparatus's legs.

With the help of Tatiana and Zanna, Rhonna started loading the Thunderstones one at a time into the artifact's egg-shaped feeding chamber.

"It's almost ready!" Rhonna shouted. She eyed the five chambers then turned to Grey Cloak. "We need your stone, donkey skull!"

"Oh." He hurried over with the Stone of Transport. He looked in the empty chamber and hesitated.

Rhonna shoved his back. "What are you waiting for? That thing to hatch?"

"Sorry." He'd grown more than fond of the stone's useful powers. He placed it inside. "Now what?"

Rhonna and the dwarves started handing out leather headgear with lenses that fit over the eyes. "Put these goggles on." She tossed a pair to Nath. "You, too, long hair. Unless you want to gawk and let your eyes burn out."

She made her way over to the ladder that led up to the seat of the apparatus. "Come on, Grey. You're seeing it through with me."

He followed her up the steps and put on his goggles. The morning sky dimmed.

Rhonna stood on her toes and started turning the handles on a pair of wheels. "You need to help me aim. Look through the scope."

"The scope?"

She pointed at the cylinder on top of the weapon. "The spyglass. We want to hit him dead center. There's an aiming point where two lines intersect. Crosshairs, they call them. Go for the chest."

He put his eye on the end of the spyglass. The crosshairs were high and far off to the right. The barrel wasn't even lined up. "We are way off. Several feet. We need to rotate right."

Rhonna shouted to the dwarves on the ground. "Rotate the turret right! Get us in the vicinity and load a pellet in the barrel!"

As the barrel swung around, the blond-bearded dwarf picked up a pellet that filled his arms like a round watermelon. He was too short to feed the tube.

"He's not tall enough," Zora said. "The nose is too high."

Dyphestive walked over to the stack of pellets, picked one up over his head, and fed it into the barrel. "It's loaded."

Black Frost walked right into the crosshairs of the Apparatus of Ruune.

"It's time to fire!" Grey Cloak looked at the goggle-faced Rhonna. "What are we waiting for?"

"The switch! Turn the switch!"

He spotted a brass dial with arcane symbols in the middle of the apparatus's strange console and turned it to the right.

The Apparatus of Ruune hummed with life. The windows where the Thunderstones nestled flickered inside the egg-shaped feeding tube and grew in brightness. It started to rotate, slow at first but quickly gaining speed. A high-pitched whine followed.

Whirrr-eeee!

Black Frost picked up speed.

"Tatiana, signal Streak and Anya!" Grey Cloak ordered. "Tell them to get clear!"

Using the Star of Light for communication, she raised it and sent out a series of pulses that shot from her hand and made a beeline for Anya. It would strike the woman with her very thoughts.

In the distance, Cinder let out a thunderous roar. The Sky Riders and Southern Storm scattered away from Black Frost.

Grey Cloak's hair stood on end. The apparatus hummed with power that permeated the cloak, his skin, and down into his bones. His voice trembled from the sonic vibrations as he called, "Now, Rhonna!"

She pointed at a twin triggers handle in the middle of the console. "Now!"

He grabbed the handles and squeezed the iron triggers.

Puh-thoom! An egg-shaped pellet of scintillating light torpedoed out of the barrel.

Grey Cloak watched as time seemed to slow down, and everyone on the tower caught their breath. Suddenly, the torpedo didn't seem so significant. Its size and shape diminished the closer it came to Black Frost. No bigger than a bright dot against his gargantuan girth, it struck.

There was a moment of silence. A bright flash followed by an ear-jarring explosion and a shockwave broke the quiet.

Black Frost's chest scales rippled from the strike like a calm pool disturbed by a large stone. He stumbled backward.

Everyone on the tower top let out a cheer.

"Load another! Load another!" Grey Cloak said, but Dyphestive had already fed it another pellet. He squeezed the trigger. Another mystic pellet rocketed out.

"Keep loading! Keep loading!"

Dyphestive fed the tube. Rhonna aimed. Grey Cloak fired.

Puh-thoom!

Puh-thoom!

Puh-thoom!

Puh-thoom!

Smoke from the battlefield rose from the ground up into the clouds. Nothing could be seen through the milky haze.

The barrel of the Apparatus of Ruune was hot as a furnace poker.

"We better let it cool," Rhonna said. "We don't want to melt the thing."

"Agreed." Grey Cloak craned his neck to spot Black Frost. He wasn't alone either. Nothing could be seen through the fog, and no sound of the dragon could be heard. It was as if everything in the world came to a stop.

Only the whine of the spinning feeding chamber carried on as everyone's eyes were glued on the thick wall of mist over one hundred yards away.

"Tell me it killed him." He'd hoped to see Black Frost dead but standing with great holes punched through his body. He looked down at Nath. "He should be dead, shouldn't he?"

Nath brushed his hair out of his eyes. "I can't imagine anything living that could survive an attack like that. In my world, it destroyed an entire city. And only with three Thunderstones at that."

The hot winds of the plains began to carry the mist away. The smoke cleared. Black Frost remained. With his hateful eyes aglow, he started to laugh.

42

Grey Cloak sank in his seat. "Was that an epic failure or what?" He caught the fallen faces of his friends looking back at him.

"It's not over yet!" Rhonna turned a brass dial on the console. "The pellets might not be working as we hoped, but we can still use a direct cannon shot."

"I remember you mentioning that back at the armory, but what does that mean?"

Nath had climbed halfway up the stairs, and from a position lower than Grey Cloak, he said, "It means that the full power of the Thunderstones has not been released yet." There were a few more metal switches on the console, five in all, each stamped with a Thunderstone's color. He flipped them in a particular order.

The artifact's chamber spun faster, brightened, and made a higher-pitched hum. The members of Talon covered their ears.

"Listen to me!" Nath shouted above the noise. "You have to let me pull the trigger!"

"Why?" Grey Cloak shouted back.

He crammed himself into the seat. "Because, with this much power, it can destroy the user entirely."

Grey Cloak nodded at Rhonna. "Go. You have your people to take care of."

"What about you and him?"

He shrugged. "I have the cloak. It can protect us."

She looked at Nath. "Are you sure you know what you're doing?"

He nodded. "I've seen the plans before. I know enough." Nath shoved his way onto the seat and helped Rhonna down the stairs. He patted her bun. "I have a dear friend, Brenwar. I think you and he'd get along."

"Is he a dwarf?"

"The best."

She said, "Maybe some other time."

Elf, man, dwarf, and dragon backed away from the glistening metal machine.

Black Frost came with a snarl on his partially grotesque face. The creases between his scales started to heat up. Steam rose from his nostrils. They felt the vapors of his hot breath from the hundred or so yards away.

Sitting hip to hip with Grey Cloak, Nath said, "Are you ready?"

"At this point, I'm ready for anything."

"Good." Nath flashed what was left of what must've been a once very dashing smile. "No matter what, don't let go. You have to hang on as long as you can, or the weapon will stop."

Grey Cloak put his hands on one trigger handle, and Nath took the other. The energy was hot to the touch and flowed through his entire body.

"Can you feel it?" Nath's jowls shook as he spoke. "The power! The elements! All in harmony! All under our command! Focus your thoughts, Grey Cloak! What do you want?"

Pure exhilaration ran through his body. "Black Frost must be destroyed!"

"Picture it happening and squeeze!"

He gave her a wink. They pulled the triggers at the same time.

The runes on the cannon pulsed spectacularly, matching the Thunderstones' colors. The apparatus hummed like a ravenous animal.

Suddenly, the weapon kicked. *Puh-thoom!*

A stream of pure light shot out of the cannon's barrel. A corded myriad of mystical colors over a foot thick buried itself in Black Frost's chest.

The titan bellowed in an earsplitting voice that shook the clouds.

"Don't let go!" Nath said.

"I won't!" His hands burned with pain. The metal contraption heated up like the inside of an oven. The cloak kept him insulated, but only so much.

Nath's scaly arms started to smoke. The scales began to stink. The tips of his frayed hair curled.

"What's happening? Why isn't it killing him?" Zora shouted from the wall. "He's still coming!"

She was right. Black Frost should have had a hole blown clean through him. Instead, step by step, he advanced. And that wasn't all.

"Nath! Are you seeing what I'm seeing?" With a horrified look, Grey Cloak watched Black Frost's ravaged face heal. His colossal size increased. "No, this can't be. Not after all of this."

He looked at Nath. The bright flecks of gold in his brown eyes had faded. "Oh no. I was afraid of that, even though I didn't believe it possible."

"What are you are talking about?"

With a forlorn look growing on his haggard face, Nath answered, "There is always a possibility that something might react the opposite of what you expect if you've never done it before. Such is the way with magic. 'Anything that can go wrong, might go wrong,' a wise man once stated.

"Black Frost has fed off my world so long that he is connected to everything. The Thunderstones should have destroyed him—they should destroy anything—but they gave him strength. I'm sorry."

"It's too late to apologize now!" His skin ripped when he tore his grip from the trigger. He stood up and shouted, "Change of plans, everybody! Summon all the dragons! Into the tower!"

"What? Why?" Zora asked.

"Because our brilliant plan backfired!" He turned and saw Nath glued to his chair, smoking hands locked on the trigger handle. "Dyphestive, fetch him!"

Dyphestive nodded.

The entirety of the Apparatus of Ruune glowed molten red. The barrel started to bow, and the egg-shaped feeding chamber wobbled out of control. The Thunderstones dried up inside as Black Frost drained all of their energy, and the egg spun to a stop.

Dyphestive yanked Nath out of the chair and slung him over his shoulder. He ran across the roof and jumped into the hatch.

Grey Cloak closed the lid right as the apparatus exploded, and he heard a gloating, invincible Black Frost laughing.

43

The heroes stood inside the Time Mural chamber, staring at the growing gargantuan form of Black Frost through the archway. Dyphestive stood alongside Grey Cloak, with Nath slung over his shoulder.

Doom came. Death approached. The last days of Gapoli neared.

Streak licked his snout with his pink lizard tongue. "Are we going to wait here and die or give him one last fight?"

"I'm all for one final glorious fight," Anya said boldly.

Grey Cloak felt Zora squeezing his hand. He lifted it to his lips and kissed it.

Tatiana was behind the Pedestal of Power, talking in hushed tones with Zanna, Dalsay, and Gossamer.

"It's not over yet." Grey Cloak hurried to them.

"Blazing steel, I couldn't even cut Black Frost's toe off."

Razor's voice carried over Tatiana's, his sword hanging in his hand. "He keeps getting bigger. How can anything living be so big? But I'd still like to take a poke at him." He looked at Anya. "Let's go get him."

"No, wait!" Grey Cloak said. "No one is going anywhere." His keen hearing had caught the gist of the wizards' conversation. They were talking about going back in time.

The option had always been in the back of Grey Cloak's mind. They'd discussed it before, but he never imagined all of their weaponized artifacts would fail. Apparently, the sorceresses felt the same way.

"This is why we haven't expended the towers reserves." Tatiana's face glistened with sweat, and her fingers adjusted the stones in the bowl as she glanced back and forth in the mural. "We don't have long. Grey Cloak, gather everyone around the mural, man and dragon. Hurry!"

"You're sending us back, aren't you?" he asked. "I thought it was too dangerous if we crossed ourselves."

"Not if we are careful not to do that very thing, but we don't know what the outcome might be."

"Are we standing here waiting to be cooked, or are we going somewhere?" Razor looked about. "And where's Gorva? I'm not going without her."

"Nor I!" Jumax said as he and Gorva entered the chamber.

"Round everyone up, and bring those dragons in through the halls," Grey Cloak ordered Dyphestive and Razor.

In a booming voice, Dyphestive shouted outside of the chamber's entrance, "Everybody, come!"

"Tatiana, go with them." Gossamer tried to gently push Tatiana aside. "Dalsay and I have spoken. He will merge with me, and we'll execute it."

"No, you won't be strong enough. You need at least three wizardry users."

In a firm but understanding voice, Dalsay said, "And they will need you if there is ever any hope of return."

His ghostly form moved into Gossamer's body. Gossamer spoke in a hollow-sounding version of Dalsay's voice. "And we have a third." He looked at Zanna.

"No, Mother, you can't!" Grey Cloak objected. "You'll all die here!"

"And so will you if you don't go." Zanna held his face in her hands. "I have faith in you, all of you. Go, Grey Cloak, and do what you do best."

"And what's that?"

She gave him a quick kiss and hugged him. "Find a way to win."

"Are we going to do this or not?" Razor said as he eyed Black Frost storm the tower. "Or are we going to watch him—"

Black Frost unleashed his flames, smothering the tower top to bottom and washing the image in the mural with blue fire.

"Now, Dalsay! Now!" Tatiana shouted.

Gossamer and Zanna joined hands. The gems in the pedestal splashed their faces in an array of lively colors. The image in the mural shifted from bright fire to darkness.

"Go!" Grey Cloak said. "Everyone inside!"

"You don't have to tell me twice! It's too hot under the collar here." Razor jumped inside, followed by Shannon and the dragons, Slick and Slicer, who snaked their way in.

Grey Cloak pushed everyone he could find. He sent Anya, Cinder, Zora, Dyphestive, and Nath through the archway. He kicked Streak in the tail end. "Don't you wait on me. Get inside!"

In twos, threes, and fours, dragon and man entered the mural. Only Grey Cloak and Tatiana remained.

The tower walls started to crumble and smoke. The floor quaked. Flames seeped through the creases. The heat became unbearable.

Grey Cloak sweated inside his cloak.

"I love you, Dalsay!" Tatianna cried as Gossamer's robes caught fire.

When Zanna started to burn, Grey Cloak called out his goodbye. "I love you, too, Mother!"

Together, he and Tatiana jumped through the archway just as its founding stone fell.

44

"I can't believe they're gone." Grey Cloak leaned against Streak, head down on his arm as he wiped his eyes. "After all we've done. Everything we tried. We still failed."

"You can't blame yourself, brother." Dyphestive squatted on the spongy ground nearby. "They died so we could live. You know that."

He sighed. "I know, but it's so hard to find any sort of victory in this flop."

Zora approached and rubbed his back. "Come on. Tatiana has found what she is looking for. The fight isn't over yet."

He nodded and pushed off Streak. "Lead the way." He looked back at his dragon. "Are you coming?"

"I'll stay out here with my siblings." Streak scanned the massive cavern's endless ceiling of stalactites. "And I could use a dip in the pond. Been a while."

"See you soon."

The Time Mural had sent the company back to Safe Haven. It was the only place in the world they'd be secure, but for how long was the question.

"Your mother believes in you. You believe in you too." Zora walked with her arm around his waist, hip to hip. "So do I."

"And I," Dyphestive said. "You'll think of something. We'd have all been dead long ago if you didn't lead us."

"It's not all on me. We all worked together." He looked down at Nath, who was lying asleep on a golden spongy bed. The man's arms and hands were blistered. "Should we wake him?"

"I fed him a potion. Let him heal," Zora said. "He's been through enough."

"Sorry, so sorry," Nath muttered. He struggled to sit up anyway.

Dyphestive lifted him by the shoulders.

"Thanks," Nath said. "I feel a little better, but the guilt is killing me." He eyed their surroundings. "Safe Haven. Huh. Feels good to be back for some reason."

"Can you walk?" Dyphestive asked.

He nodded and slung his hair away from his face. "I'd be ashamed if I couldn't."

Zora broke away from Grey Cloak and came to Nath's side. "Let me help. After all, you saved me once before. It's the least I could do."

"So sweet." Nath cleared his scratchy throat. His voice deepened. "Thank you."

As they wandered toward the huge mouth that was the

entrance to the Vault, Grey Cloak struggled to close out the thoughts of the events that had transpired earlier. Zanna, Gossamer, and, he assumed, Dalsay had been destroyed by Black Frost's flame, and the tower with them. He imagined that Bowbreaker and the elves, along with the dwarves in Dwarf Skull, would be wiped out as well. Lythlenion and Crane also had been left behind. And that was only the beginning. His jaw clenched.

There has to be a way to kill that monster! Why can't we find it?

They made it inside the Vault, which was fully stocked with pristine armor and weapons and rations that could feed an army.

Anya was inside with Cinder, loading his harness and saddle with more weapons. The striking sun-bleached blonde known as Fiery Red nodded at them.

Gorva showed off her skill with a halberd while Jumax watched in admiration. Razor was nowhere to be found.

Tatiana was inside the rearmost chamber, working behind the Eye of the Sky Riders with an intense look on her face. Rhonna and her four dwarfsmen stood nearby, as well as Shannon, who greeted them as they approached.

"So, has Tatiana had any epiphanies?" Grey Cloak asked.

Shannon shrugged as she flipped a dagger over in her hand then sheathed it. She drew and repeated the process. "If she has, she hasn't shared them with me."

Grey Cloak spotted a hint of a smile growing on Tatiana's face. He joined her. "I'm not used to seeing that look, but I like it. Did it work?"

Tatiana took a deep breath and let it out. She hugged him. "Their sacrifice was not for naught. They did it."

"Did what?" Dyphestive asked.

"They sent us back in time, but when is the question. A week, a month, a year," Grey Cloak said.

"No, much farther than that. It is what we hoped our reserves would accomplish as a last resort." Tatiana broke away from Nath. "This is why your mother stayed behind. She had intimate knowledge of the one time and place that might give us a chance. The only question was, would they be able to do it. We'd never sent someone so far back in time before. That's why we tested it by sending her back to see Bowbreaker."

"How far back are we talking?" Grey Cloak asked.

"According to the Eye of the Sky Rider, the year 5999."

He titled his head. "Why does that seem familiar?"

"Because," Anya said as she strolled into the chamber, "it's the year my parents died. It's the time of the Day of Betrayal."

Grey Cloak and Dyphestive exchanged glances.

"So our parents are still alive?" the brutish blond asked.

"At this point in time, everyone is." Tatiana worked the Eye of the Sky Rider. "As we speak, the Sky Riders are at Hidemark on Gunder Island, preparing their final assault on Black Frost. We can warn of the treachery that might befall them, but we cannot let them know who we are. The timelines are delicate. It could do more unspeakable harm than good."

"That won't be easy." Grey Cloak recalled his training at Hidemark. "You know how hardheaded they are. Even if we warn them, we still need a weapon that can kill Black Frost. And we've tried everything."

"One step at a time, brother." Dyphestive laid a hand on his shoulder. "Let's go save our parents."

45

Hidden in the depths of Lake Flugen, Safe Haven might as well have been a back door to Gunder Island. With the aid of a breathing spell cast by Tatiana, the heroes made it up to the surface of the lake. The dragons swam like ducks, their heads, necks, and wings above the water.

Grey Cloak and Zora rode Streak and led from the front along with Anya and Cinder. Swimming through the choppy waters, they talked back and forth with Tatiana and Dyphestive, who both rode on Rock.

"Gunder Island will have watchful eyes," Anya warned. "They won't hesitate to strike if they spot us and suspect us as spies."

"We'll have to convince them. It won't be easy without being able to explain who we are," Tatiana said.

"Perhaps our gear will help them change their minds,"

Grey Cloak said. "After all, we wear the equipment of the Sky Riders. And we can share the knowledge of Safe Haven, can't we?"

"No, Safe Haven was created after the Day of Betrayal," Tatiana replied. "It's a matter of who we can trust. Anya, who would you speak with first?"

"I'd reach out to my uncle, Justus. Or any of the last of the Sky Riders. Perhaps Yuri Gnomeknower. She'd be one to understand."

The party swapped many ideas back and forth.

Zora asked Grey Cloak, "Tell me more about the Day of Betrayal. My memory is vague on the subject."

He leaned back and turned his head halfway around. "I studied the details when I went through my training. Before that treacherous day, Black Frost had grown in power and had secured a hold on Dark Mountain's temple. A third of the Sky Rider forces that had sided with him became the Riskers. But the faithful Sky Riders outmatched them. Or so they thought.

"The Sky Riders, with superior strength in numbers, chose to storm the castle, so to speak. What they didn't know was that Black Frost's influence had already tainted the hearts of half of the remaining Sky Riders sworn to fight against him. When they invaded Dark Mountain, the battle turned for the worse when the Sky Riders were attacked by their kindred. With two-thirds of the Sky Riders under Black Frost's control, the true Sky Riders didn't stand a chance. They were slaughtered, and only a handful escaped with their lives."

"We will have vengeance this day!" Anya tightened her grip

on her hilt. "My sword will drink the blood of those backstabbing cowards!"

The dragons came to a stop half a league from the shores of Gunder Island. Its tropical green flora flourished, and vibrant flowers and bushes speckled the vibrant landscape. A mountainous hill encircled a hidden valley where the Sky Riders did their training. High in the sky, dragon scouts circled the island.

"I'm going to go in alone," Grey Cloak said.

"What?" Anya replied. "If anyone—"

"No, listen to me. You need to lead our forces to Dark Mountain and wait in case I can't convince them. They'll need the aid if the fight begins, and only then will they know we are on their side." Grey Cloak turned all the way around in his saddle to face Zora. He pinched the Scarf of Shadows. "Might I borrow this?"

"Of course." Zora untied it and placed it around his neck. "What's mine is yours. But I'm not leaving."

"Nor am I," Streak said. "I'll be ready for your call."

"Brother, I insist on coming with you," Dyphestive pleaded.

"Even though your stealth skills are unrivaled? I'll have to insist you stay." He smirked. "They need you more than me for the fight this time, brother."

Dyphestive nodded. "I understand."

Grey Cloak kissed Zora, waved goodbye, then dove into the waters.

With the speed of the fleetest fish, the Cloak of Legends propelled Grey Cloak. He cut through the waters and made it to shore in no time. He crossed the beach, shed his boots, then sped up the mountainside using his gift of speed.

By the time he crested the hilltop, he was barely winded. He looked down into the enclosed valley of tall trees and a landscape thick with colorful vegetation.

Hmm...

The dragon scouts weren't the only creatures with prying eyes. Scattering birds caused problems. The elven sisters, Stayzie and Mayzie, had taught him that during his Sky Rider training. He lifted the Scarf of Shadows to his nose.

If I only had the Stone of Transport. A shame it was destroyed.

He descended into the valley and traversed the faint pathways that wound through the forest to where the entrance to Hidemark waited. It didn't appear any different than when he'd done his training. Only that time, in the courtyard, two hundred Sky Riders and their dragons were in military formation, receiving orders from the valiant-looking Justus, Anya's uncle.

The well-knit warrior's long chestnut hair hung down over his shoulder plates. His beard, peppered with white, was well-trimmed. Justus wasn't the only familiar Sky Rider he saw.

It's Hogrim, Gorva's father, and Slomander. Stayzie, Mayzie, and Arik still live! There's Hammerjaw—no mistaking that black-bearded dwarf's big belly.

His gaze swept through the ranks, where he spied many new faces. He didn't see any signs of Yuri Gnomeknower. *I know where she'll be.*

Keeping his distance from the Sky Rider ranks, Grey Cloak stole his way inside the vaulted temple-like entrance of Hidemark. The ancient sanctuary's high ceilings and wide hallways led him straight back to Yuri's study. He found her inside the alcove, sitting in a chair made from the white belly of a lizard, with her eyes closed.

He crept closer and started to speak.

"Ah, an intruder." She opened her eyes and looked right at him. "Did you come to kill me?"

46

Yuri was a fuzzy-faced gnome with wizened features and crinkly skin. On the small side, she wore a modest set of wizard robes and soft shoes underneath. Her short arms were folded across her chest, and her large eyes probed him from head to toe.

"Methinks you came to slay me." Her scarred and gnarled hands reached for a straight wooden walking cane. It floated from a work table and into her hand. "You'll find I'm not so easy a mark as you think."

Grey Cloak showed the palms of his hands. "No, Yuri, you don't understand. I am a friend. I've come to warn you of the danger of the mission to Dark Mountain."

"Oh?" She raised an eyebrow. "Then you won't mind me doing this." She flicked her wrist with her cane in hand. A ring of energy snared Grey Cloak and squeezed.

"Fine," he grunted. "But will you let me make my case?"

She left the chair and approached. "I have to admit, I am curious, even though you bear the clothing of an assassin." She eyed his clothing. "Subtle. Indistinguishable. One who blends in."

"If an assassin wanted to blend in, he'd dress like a Sky Rider, wouldn't he?"

Yuri raised another eyebrow at that. "He'd have a silver tongue too."

"Please, hear me out."

She rubbed her jaw. "I'm listening, but make it quick."

"You are heading for a trap. Half of your Sky Rider forces are going to betray you."

"Preposterous." She busted him in the knee with her cane. "All Sky Riders are sworn by their duty."

He dropped to his knees even though the Cloak of Legends protected him. He grunted, faking the pain. "If that is the case, then how did Black Frost come to betray you? How did a third of the Sky Riders turn their backs in the first place?"

Yuri's lips tightened. "You make a valid point. Who are you? And what did you mean that you're a friend?"

"What I am about to tell you will seem impossible to believe, but I am Jerrik and Zanna Paydark's son, Grey Cloak, er, I mean Dindae."

"I see the resemblance to her and Jerrik, but that means nothing. You're hiding something."

Grey Cloak sighed. It seemed the only way to convince the

shrewd gnome would be to tell her the entire story. He would have to trust her. "You're right."

"Go on."

He started from Talon's journey through Time Mural and worked his way back to Black Frost's rise in power.

After he'd finished, Yuri leaned on her cane and considered him. "I feel no deception in your words, but how can I be sure that what you're saying is true?"

He nodded. "How else do I know about my mother's secret mission? She is using the battle at Dark Mountain as a distraction to destroy the portal that my father helped create. Black Frost's trap is set. There are betrayers among you."

"Or," a man said in a strong voice, "you are a filthy spy, sent to distract us from our quest."

Grey Cloak turned his head as soon as he saw Yuri's eyes grow bigger.

Five Sky Riders in full gear blocked the alcove exit with their Sky Blades in hand. One of them was Justus, but he didn't recognize the two women and two men with him.

Justus rested his blade on Grey Cloak's shoulder and touched the razor-sharp edge to his neck. "Did you really think you could slip into Hidemark unnoticed? Over a dozen dragons sniffed you out."

"Eliminate him, Justus," a human woman with one blue eye and one green said. "We are on borrowed time. We need to execute our plan with no distractions."

"This young man has committed no offense to me," Yuri

stated with narrowed eyes. "You are always quick to shed blood, Stanya."

Stanya? It was just as Anya had said. Her parents were still alive.

Grey Cloak noted the similarities between the woman who wanted to kill him and his friend Anya. They even sounded the same. He kept his tongue tied, however. Chances were that if Stanya wasn't working with the Riskers, the other three were.

Justus frowned at Yuri. "So, what did this intruder tell you?"

Yuri quickly relayed Grey Cloak's claims about traitors in their ranks but left out the chunk about the time travel.

"This again?" Justus sheathed his sword. "No doubt this is the work of Black Frost's chameleons. But there is only one way to be certain. Take him to the dungeons. Unleash a flayer and let it do the work on him like the last one. We'll deal with him when we return—if there is anything left to speak with."

Grey Cloak turned to Justus. "You must listen to me. Even Black Frost could not come up with such a far-fetched story."

In a stern voice, Justus said, "Black Frost is desperate. His forces are outnumbered, and he knows his last hours are coming. The Sky Riders are united, as always."

"Nice try." Stanya stepped over to Grey Cloak and removed his scarf. She slugged him in the gut. "But you won't be needing this anymore, trickster." She tossed it to Yuri. "Destroy this."

Two of the other Sky Riders hooked him by the arms and lifted him from the ground.

"Yuri, please believe me. You have to convince them my

words are true," he said as they dragged him away. "The Sky Riders are too proud. That is their weakness. Black Frost exploits—*mmph!*"

One of the Sky Riders, a lizard man, stuffed a rag in his mouth and bound it all the way around his head. "Sssilence," the lizardman hissed.

"That's not going to do any good," the other Sky Rider, an orc, said. "He's a chatty one." He drew a dagger and cocked it back. "This will do it."

The last thing Grey Cloak saw as he was dragged out of the alcove was Yuri's curious eyes peering at him. Then his head exploded in bright stars, followed by blackness.

"Ugh," Grey Cloak moaned as he came to. He rubbed the throbbing lump on the back of his head then crawled across the damp floor into a sitting position behind the wall.

The cell was stone from floor to ceiling, with a grid of solid metal bars walling off the exit. The locking mechanism on the door was sealed from the inside and otherwise couldn't be seen.

"Zooks. I need to figure out how long I've been in here."

"It won't matter." The Sky Rider posted at the outside of the door showed his rugged half-orc face. "You'll be dead soon enough, chameleon."

"I'm not a chameleon."

"Sure, you aren't." The hard-eyed orc looked above Grey Cloak.

Grey Cloak glanced above. A horrid creature that made his skin crawl slithered around the ceiling. He scooted as far away as possible, huddling in the corner. "Tell me that's not a flayer."

"Oh, it's a flayer. And it's going to feed on your skull all night." He grinned. "And I'm going to watch."

47

The flayer was a slimy, inky green. It slinked across the ceiling like a dripping underwater sea creature. Its many tentacles spread out and rippled as it moved, each stretchy leg making a sucking sound as it moved closer. Spitlike gobs dropped from its tendrils to the stone floor. In the middle was a ring of gums with thousands of teeth that could swallow Grey Cloak's head whole. A dozen watery, bloodshot eyes encircled the mouth and fixed on him.

Grey Cloak wasn't entirely without his defenses. He reached inside his cloak, pulled out a dagger, and summoned his wizard fire.

"Say!" The guard started. "Where'd you get that? We searched you thoroughly. I did it myself."

"Apparently, you aren't as skilled as you think. Judging by

your looks, you aren't very skilled at all. Or even a natural." He gave a triumphant smirk. "You're in over your head."

"I think you are the one over your head," the Sky Rider said with a snarl. He crossed his arms, propped his foot up against the adjacent wall, and leaned back. "You aren't going anywhere. No tricks can fool the flayer. Nor me."

Grey Cloak fired a shot of energy into the flayer. Its fleshy body rippled. It kept coming, faster this time.

"Ha!" The guard slapped his knee. "Flayers are immune to magic attacks. That's what makes them so powerful."

Grey Cloak put more oomph into the next blast. The flayer didn't slow. It reached the ceiling directly above him, and he had to move from spot to spot, evading the nasty thing.

"This will be interesting. At least you are putting up a better fight than the last chameleon." The guardian moved out of sight and reappeared with a skull in his hands. "This is all that's left of the last prisoner." He stuck his finger through a hole in the top of the skull. "Sucked the gray matter right out as soon as we had what we wanted."

Grey Cloak's stomach flipped. *Zooks. This is getting serious.*

To make matters worse, the flayer began to stretch-out out, covering the ceiling from corner to corner. It started to seep down.

He grabbed the bars. "Let me out of here! You have to believe me—the Sky Riders are in danger. Black Frost has set a trap. I can prove it."

The Sky Rider tossed the skull up and down, looked toward

the exit at the end of the aisle. "Heh, I know that. Why do you think we're killing you?"

Grey Cloak cringed as he looked up at the gooey ceiling that began to drip. The flayer's jaws replicated and made snapping-sucking sounds. "I thought you only wanted information. Why kill me? Justus wouldn't approve of that."

"Oh, you are right. Justus certainly wouldn't approve of such a foul act, but Justus isn't Justus. He's the chameleon." The half orc made a rough chuckle. "Now you understand why you have to die." He kicked the skull down the hall. "I don't know how you sniffed out our plan, but before you die, we'll figure it out."

The flayer's mouths started to ooze and stretch down from the ceiling.

Grey Cloak crouched. His only hope was that the cloak would protect him, but that wouldn't get him out of the cell. He reached inside his inner pockets and pulled out the Figurine of Heroes.

Desperate times, desperate measures. If this comes back to bite me, I'm doomed.

Eyeballing the figurine, the guard grabbed the spear leaning against the wall. "What's that? Give it to me."

"You'll find out soon enough." Grey Cloak whispered the command word. "*Osid-ayan-umra-shokrah-ha!*" He tossed the figurine through the bars. It hit the floor in the aisle and remained upright. A swirl of black-and-gray smoke spit out of the figurine's head, clouding the hall.

The guard started coughing. "Broken horseshoes! What

treachery is this?" He fumbled through the mist and vanished from sight.

Grey Cloak flattened himself on his belly and locked his fingers together.

Please come to my aid. No more surprises.

The guard reappeared, fumbling around in the dispersing smoke. He rubbed his eyes, coughed a few times, and blinked. But another person stood among the thinning mist. A very lean man, pale-skinned with a floppy cap hanging over one side of his face. He wore a plum-colored vest and a dull gold shirt underneath with the long, baggy sleeves buttoned up. His bony fingers had little meat on them. One hand was empty, and the other carried what looked like a metal carafe of wine. A deep frown enhanced the dimple in his chin.

"Look at you," the guard said as he lowered his spear. "A man as brittle as a stick. Who are you? His savior?"

The stranger gave the half orc a steely look before he glanced at Grey Cloak. "I'm Melegal, and I'm not pleased that someone interrupted my affairs. Who do I have to blame for this?"

Grey Cloak wiggled his fingers.

"Ah, I see." He touched his exposed ear underneath his salt-and-pepper hair. "A lot of strange points on ears of late. There wouldn't happen to be any pointy-eared ladies around? They are quite fetching."

The guard lunged at him with his spear.

Melegal sidestepped out of the way and clamped his free hand on the half orc's metal bracers. "A full suit of metal armor? Shiny too. How nice and absolutely perfect."

The guard responded by throwing a punch. "I'll bust your teeth out, lip flapper!"

Bzzt! The half orc's entire body shook, and his armor suit rattled. He wobbled on his legs then fell face-first on the stones.

"Well done!" Grey Cloak crawled away from the descending mouths of ooze. "Do you think you could help me out of here? After all, that's why I summoned you."

Melegal faced the bars and twisted the metal signet ring on his ring finger. "I'm not so sure my band will work on that." He sawed his long finger under his lip. "What did you say your name was?"

"Grey Cloak."

"Interesting. Juvenile but interesting." Melegal took a long draw from his carafe.

"Please, Melegal, what are you waiting for?"

The roguishly handsome man shrugged. "Give me a moment. I make better decisions when I've been drinking."

48

When Melegal turned his carafe over, not a single drop was left. Satisfied, he rubbed his little potbelly and squatted down. "I've come to a decision."

Grey Cloak was bundled up in his cloak with ooze spreading all over him. "One way or the other, will you act on it immediately?"

"Certainly." Melegal reached behind him, searched the guard, then grabbed a key ring. He traced his finger over the key's teeth. "Not very sophisticated." He tossed the key ring down the hall and removed a leather case from inside his vest. He locked his fingers, flexed his knuckles, then cracked them. "I could use the practice. It's been a while."

"Please, hurry!" The Cloak of Legends throbbed like an aching heart. The creature invading it had a powerfully strange impact.

Melegal stuck two metal tools in the lock and said, "You are dressed like a thief or assassin. Shrouded in a cloak. I respect your subtle panache. I'd think you'd be able to make your way around this mechanism, but the locking plate would be difficult to reach without dislocating some bones."

"Not to mention the guard with a spear keeping me at a distance."

"True. The brutes are always such a nuisance."

The lock popped open. He swung the door wide and stepped aside. "Please, don't get anything gooey on me. It's my favorite ensemble, and the wife keeps trying to burn it."

Grey Cloak sprang out of the door.

The tendrils clung to the throbbing cloak then finally tore away.

Melegal slammed the door shut, but the flayer seeped between the bars. He backed away, and the flayer changed course toward the guard. "Let it feed on orcface. More meat on the bones."

They put more distance between themselves and the flayer. Grey Cloak grabbed the figurine, and they made their way toward the dungeon's exit door.

He turned to Melegal. "Thank you."

Melegal tipped his cap. "There wouldn't be a wine cellar nearby, would there? I'll accept that as payment." He started to fade. "Pish, just when it started to get interesting." His body turned into vapors, and he was gone.

Grey Cloak put away the figurine and headed up the steps.

He opened the door and found himself face-to-face with Yuri Gnomeknower. "Zooks."

"Don't be alarmed," the wizened gnome said. "I know everything."

"How's that?"

She flicked her gnarled cane left and right. From the corner of the ceiling halfway down the hall to his cell, a giant eyeball with bat wings and spider legs dropped into the corridor.

"A yonder. How'd I miss that?" he said as it flew toward him. "I thought they only existed in Monarch City."

Yuri shook her head. "I *borrowed* this one and made some modifications." She let it land on her shoulder. "I gave it cute little ears."

He noticed the fuzzy buttonholes in front of the wings. "So, you heard what the guard said?"

"Every word. Something has been gnawing at my belly, and now I know what it is. Justus is a shape changer, and if that is the case, the real Justus is probably dead."

"No, I don't think so. In the future, he fought to the very end when Black Frost invaded Gunder Island. He must have been alive somehow. Is there anywhere else they might have taken him?"

Yuri's brow furrowed. "Chameleons are known to keep their enemies alive to replicate them more precisely. Perhaps Justus is nearby. Right under our noses, in plain sight. After all, no one comes to these dungeons aside for rare occasions. We'll search the cells."

Back down the corridor, the flayer had completely coated the guard's body. It made awful sucking sounds. Grey Cloak tried not to look. "How about you take this corridor?"

Yuri patted the yonder on the top of its head, and with a warm smile, she said, "He'll handle it. I'll take the right, and you can take the left. There are only three aisles."

The cells were unmolested, the floors clean and the metal bars polished. Even the cots were in fine shape.

Grey Cloak hurried down the aisle, swinging his gaze from side to side and making his way all the way to the back. He found a man hanging in the very last cell. "Justus! Yuri, I found him!"

Justus was stripped down to his trousers. His muscular frame was chained to the wall, and he'd been blindfolded and gagged. Red striped his body, and blood caked his chest and the floor. If he breathed, he didn't show it.

Yuri arrived and tossed Grey Cloak the key ring. He opened the cell.

"Oh, Justus, what have they done to you?" She smacked her cane against the chains.

Grey Cloak caught the man as he fell from the wall and lowered him to the floor. He removed the blindfold and gag. "He breathes, thank the dragons."

"Carry him to my study." Yuri hustled out of the cell. "I'll tend to him there."

49

"It all makes sense," Justus said. He sat in a chair in Yuri's alcove, head down, rubbing his temples. His hair hung over his eyes, and he swept it away when he leaned back. "We are in great debt to you, Grey Cloak, son of Zanna Paydark. As remarkable as your story is, I believe it."

Yuri handed Grey Cloak the Scarf of Shadows and the Rod of Weapons. "Justus, now that we know, how will we warn the faithful? And how do we know who the faithful are?"

"Only the heat of battle can tell." The strong-jawed Justus stood up. "I'm going to suit up." He dropped his gaze to Grey Cloak. "You say Cinder has children that will come to our aid?"

"Yes."

"And they are near?"

"Only my dragon, Streak. The flight will be crowded, but we can do it."

Justus's jaw tightened. "To think, an imposter rides my dragon. Firestok should know better." His fists clenched. "Summon your dragon. Meet me in the square."

Outside, in front of the temple, Yuri and Grey Cloak waited on Streak.

"I've never seen Hidemark abandoned," Yuri said. "The full force of the Sky Riders is gone, and that's not typical."

"No, Black Frost is determined to wipe all of them out at once." He kept his eyes skyward. "But a remnant always survives. You and Justus were among them, and you trained me." He spotted a dragon-shaped speck in the sky coming from the south, buzzing the tops of the trees on the rim. "Ah, there he is."

Yuri squinted. "I thought you said there was one dragon, but I see two."

"You're right." Streak came in fast, but he wasn't alone. Grey Cloak laughed. "Slick is with him."

"You sound surprised."

"I shouldn't be. Apparently, Anya left another dragon behind. She has difficulty following orders from me. Her intentions and instincts are good, albeit a tad aggressive at times."

"Sounds like her mother, Stanya."

Streak appeared with Zora on his back, then Slick landed.

"It's about time," Streak said. "My scales were getting waterlogged."

Yuri touched both dragons' snouts. "Beautiful. Ha! The sons of Cinder and Firestok, all grown up. Wonderful." She looked up at Zora. "And who is this?"

"I'm Zora." She reached down and shook Yuri's hand. "You

must be Yuri Gnomeknower. Grey Cloak has told me a little bit about you."

"Aye. I can imagine it's confusing." She turned her attention to Grey Cloak. "I'm not informed about the intricacies of the Time Mural of which you speak, but I assume we must work with each other using great discretion."

Grey Cloak nodded. "Tatiana of the Wizard Watch has spoken to all of us about it, men and dragon alike. We will do our best to limit our contact with, eh, family, so to speak." Grey Cloak joined Zora in the saddle. "My concern is finding a way to destroy Black Frost. All of our efforts failed in the future. Yuri, we need to find a way."

While they waited, he described the extent of Black Frost's size and power.

Yuri's crinkly skin paled. "We never could have thought his strength would be so vast." She gave him a worried look. "He decimated the Wizard Watch? Unbelievable."

"He wiped out Hidemark too," Grey Cloak said with a grim expression. "He did it during my Sky Rider training." Gunder Island was supposed to have had the perfect protection from Black Frost. His forces hadn't wanted to tangle with the giants that protected this land. But it hadn't been enough against the dragon himself. Even Garthar, the giant's supreme leader, and his thick skin and great size had been no match for Black Frost. "Like a cloud that covered the canyon, Black Frost appeared. No dragon flame was a match for his fire. He burned the remaining Sky Riders to a crisp. Anya and I were the only ones to survive, as we weren't present."

"And if you hadn't survived," Yuri said gravely, "the rest of the world would have been gone with that attack."

At that moment, Justus exited Hidemark's temple entrance in a full suit of polished dragon-scale plate armor. He carried an open-faced, winged helmet in the nook of one arm and a curled bugle made out of dragon horn in the other. "This isn't my suit. The fiend apparently borrowed mine." He wiggled inside the metal. "A little tight to my liking." He spotted Zora. "And who is this lovely vision?" He kissed her hand. "I am Justus."

She blushed. "Zora."

"A pleasure." Justus turned to the dragons. "And look at these striking creatures. Sons of Cinder. Magnificent."

"I'm Slick. Saddle up, Justus. I'm eager to see my mother."

Justus stroked the scales on his neck. "Odd circumstances. We'll have to make it work out." He climbed into the saddle. "Lead the way, Grey Cloak, and fill me in. Apparently, we have a great deal to contemplate if we are going to upend Black Frost."

"Ride the sky," Grey Cloak said.

"Lords of the Air!" Justus shouted as Yuri joined him on Slick's back. "Let our wings be swift and the wind carry us to plateaus unreached!"

With her hands resting on his waist, Zora said to Grey Cloak, "You've been very quiet. What's racing through that mind of yours?"

"Saving the world and everyone in it."

"Grey, it's not all on you. Don't overburden yourself." She massaged his shoulders. "You're tight as a drum skin."

He shrugged. "Are you telling me to relax? The notion escapes me. Everything we've tried has failed, and now, we're boldly rushing into another battle without a suitable plan. Or weapon."

She tapped a finger on his head. "What is in here is the best weapon. And you don't have to come up with it alone. You might be the leader, but you have help." She looked over at Justus and Yuri, who were talking back and forth. "And the wisdom of some elders. You'll think of something."

"At this point, I'm fresh out of ideas."

"Then *we'll* think of something."

As confident as Grey Cloak was at escaping death, he'd yet to find a way to evade the inevitable. Another battle with Black Frost, facing superior strength and a superior force. Back when he'd trained to be a Sky Rider, they'd instilled in the adepts that no foe, no matter how strong, large, or intelligent, was invincible. They had a saying back then. "Flesh and bone. Steel and stones. We bring defeat."

In the case of Black Frost, they'd yet to find a way to stop him. At the present moment, Black Frost wasn't at his full strength. He would be vulnerable. With superior numbers and command of energies from another world, the wicked dragon's defenses would be nigh impossible to pierce.

Grey Cloak wrestled with his thoughts. *I know he can be beaten.* He could feel it on the tip of his tongue, but the words escaped him. *Zooks, Grey Cloak, we are so close. Think of something!*

50

Grey Cloak and company rendezvoused with Dyphestive, Anya, and the rest of Talon in the bleak black hills north of Ugrad's borders.

Anya and her uncle, Justus, had an awkward reunion in which he told her how grown up and beautiful she'd become. Next, they mapped out the battleground in the cold dirt, and she recalled what she knew of the original battle that had been passed down to her from Justus.

"The plan was to overcome Black Frost's forces and confront him at the temple, the source of his power." She set down a chipped-up hunk of stone. Using acorns, they mapped out the location of the dragons and placed them around the stone. "As you can see, the Sky Riders have superior numbers." Using a stick, she pointed at the mass of acorns south of the temple. "But when the battle started in the sky, a third of the Sky Riders peeled off."

Justus started dividing the acorns in the southern position. "So the traitors turned back to box the Sky Riders in from the north and south?" He looked at Anya. "The perfect ambush, but even we would have anticipated such an attempt. Or at least, I'd like to think I would have."

"But you aren't you," Anya said.

He nodded.

Grey Cloak stepped beside Anya and squatted down. "I remember my mother telling me they'd discussed the worst possible scenarios, but the ambush was cast aside. They still felt the battle would serve as a decoy to slip behind Black Frost's defenses, enter the temple, and destroy the portal."

"Whose idea was that?" Justus asked.

He looked him dead in the eye. "Yours."

"Nature's call! I've played a hand in all of this." He stood and stomped the acorns representing Black Frost. "Who could have imagined this battle would lead to the destruction of Gapoli? We must end this menace before he decimates us again!"

"Don't fret, uncle. This time we know what they are planning. That gives us an edge. We only need to figure out how to confuse them before they attack tomorrow."

Justus locked his fingers behind his head. "How do we know that there is not a traitor among us?" He eyed everyone. "At this moment?"

"A fair question, but we have no choice but to trust each

other and act on faith now," Grey Cloak said. "Think about it, you've never seen a one of us before, or most of us."

"I pray you are the true son of Zanna Paydark," Justus said. "Tell me something only your mother would know about me."

"You refuse to eat your oats cold," Grey Cloak said, "and if it helps, it was you two, my father, and Olgstern who set up Safe Haven in secret. Hopefully, that puts some ghosts to rest."

"Ha! You are right!" Justus grabbed his shoulders. "You know my oldest of friends!"

Grey Cloak's wheels started to turn. "If enough of us can get a clear shot at Black Frost, at this early stage, I believe we can take him down. The trick is penetrating his forces. We'll need to confuse the Riskers when they attack." He scooped over some new acorns and put them in the field of play. "Justus, the Sky Riders listen to your voice. They won't know the difference between you and your imposter. If we secretly take out the chameleon, perhaps we can deter their betrayal and buy time."

Justus crossed his arms. "I like it. Keep talking, son of Zanna."

"The issue is separating the good Sky Riders from the bad. If we can avoid the ambush, draw Black Frost's forces out—" he shifted around the acorns "—we'll have a clear path to him and the temple. That still leaves us with the issue of destroying the dragon. I don't know whether any of our weapons will do enough damage against him. His scales are as steel plating, and he's far larger than any of our grands."

"Brother, if I can get a clean strike, the Iron Sword will take his head off," Dyphestive said.

"Son of Olgstern Stronghair, I'm in line with your thinking." Justus's eyes shone with admiration. "Your father would be proud to see you wield it."

"The one thing about Black Frost is, he's prepared for anything. Getting such a strike will be slim, and we can't assume that it will be a success. We need another plan." Grey Cloak set an acorn on the rock that represented the temple. "Every weapon we have tried has failed. The Helm of the Dragons. The Apparatus of Ruune. What will it take to break him?" He noticed the chains linked together on Streak's harness. He tilted his head over one shoulder. "Huh."

"Huh, what?" Anya asked.

Zora smiled. "I think he thought of something."

51

Talon contemplated stealing their way into the Sky Rider camp and kidnapping the chameleon posing as Justus. Then Justus could resume his position. The majority, including Grey Cloak and Anya, agreed that was too risky. They came up with another plan instead, but that time, Grey Cloak objected.

"Zora, I can't let you do this. I know that Scarf of Shadows is yours, but I can't bear the thought of anything happening to you." He fastened his hands on her wrists. There are over two hundred dragons and their riders. They sniffed me out at Hidemark, and they'll sniff you out as well."

"No, they won't. You aren't as smart as me." She gave him a smirk as Gorva and Tatiana rubbed dragon oil all over his clothing and bare skin like perfume. "Not that dragons stink, but do I even want to know where this comes from?"

Gorva answered, "Don't even try to guess." Her nostrils flared. "Even though it should be obvious."

"We'll remain close to her," Jumax said. He put a strong hand on Grey Cloak's shoulder. "If there is danger, we will stage the rescue, Grey One. You have your mission. We have ours."

"He's right," Zora said. "Your plan won't work if you are not at the front. Even if I don't survive, you will still have hope. After all, they'll never figure out what I am trying to do."

They embraced. Grey Cloak swallowed her up in his arms and didn't want to let go. "Dragon's speed, Zora."

She kissed his cheek with very soft lips. "To you as well."

Justus walked over. "Fair one, this is the battle horn. Find the one in my imposter's possession and stuff this deep inside the bell." He handed her a leather wrap filled with gummy wax mixed with dead leaves and tiny twigs. "When he blows it to signal the betrayal, it will not work, and then I shall use my horn to take command before the battle." He eyed Grey Cloak. "It is a sound plan. I wish I thought of it myself."

"Do well, Zora." Tatiana gave her a quick embrace. "I have faith in you."

"Yeah." Razor rocked back and forth on his heels. "Smell you later."

"Come, we must go," Gorva said.

The three of them climbed onto Smash then departed.

I never thought I'd say this, but I miss her already. Grey Cloak watched them head east toward the Sky Rider camp.

"She's in good hands, brother. You'll see her soon." Dyphestive guided Grey Cloak over to Streak. "We need to move through the night if we are to have a head start before the battle tomorrow."

"I know. It's my plan." He looked over his shoulder. "I guess I've gotten used to her riding with me."

"Straighten your back," Anya said as she walked by. "It's time for war. Get ready for it."

DRAGONS. Not in twos. Not in fours. Not baker's dozens nor scores but hundreds lay in the field. Among them were Sky Riders. Some huddled over campfires and talked quietly, and others slept on the hard ground, not a one under a blanket.

Zora crawled down from the rise where's she'd been peeking. "Gorva, did you see all of them?"

"I'd have to be blind not to. You can do it, but I will if you want me to."

"No, I'm going." She spied over the rise again. "Any idea where the chameleon will be?"

"The center."

Zora nodded. "That's where I'll be."

"If you encounter any trouble, run like a bat out of the Flaming Fence to us. We'll be watching."

Zora lifted the Scarf of Shadows over her nose and took off over the rise.

The edge of the camp was no more than fifty yards away, and it didn't take long to reach the perimeter. She stopped near a dragon just a few feet away. Her heartbeat hammered against her temples. Sky Riders slept against their dragons, who lay on the ground like boulders.

Like a cat on the prowl, she breached the camp and stole her way toward the center, traversing by scales, armor, and hot breath. *I can't believe I'm doing this.*

To her fortune, the hard-packed ground didn't leave any tracks. Only the armor-laden Sky Riders and heavy dragon paws left prints among the dirt.

The light-footed woman made it toward the middle, where a small canvas tent was set up in the open field. A beautiful grand dragon slept in front of the entrance, eyes closed and horns laying to the side.

Rogues of Rodden, she'd guarding the entrance. Zora moved to the back of the tent. The ropes and pegs were firmly tacked down. She went for her dagger.

I could cut a slit, but that might dispel the scarf. Anvils, what should I do? I have to get in there!

She put her ear against the tent. Someone moved inside. She had to take a closer look. Zora lay down on her side, lifted up a loose spot in the bottom of the tent's wall, and peeked inside.

A man lay half covered by a blanket, reading a small scroll by candlelight. His bare back was to her. His skin was pale, almost translucent, and blue veins showed underneath his skin. Unlike the real Justus, he didn't have a strand of hair on his bald head.

Ew. That's nasty.

The chameleon shifted around. His bright, piercing eyes swept the tent. "Who is there?" he said in a low and sinister voice. "I sense something." His long bony hands clutched the dragon charm that hung from his neck. He scanned the tent again.

Zora's heart beat so loud she swore the entire camp could hear it. She kept her limbs stiff and refused to move. *Calm down, Zora, calm down. Look for the bugle.*

The armor and sword belt were easy to spot. Aside from those and his blanket, there was no sign of the horn.

All of a sudden, the chameleon's body started to contort and shift into Justus. With a blanket wrapped around his waist, he exited through the tent flap.

Zora squirted under the tent and made another sweep of the confined quarters. *Dirty chipmunks, it's not here!*

She heard the chameleon's muffled voice outside, speaking to the dragon. With one last look, she slipped out under the tent's wall right as the chameleon returned.

Sweat dripped in her eye. She thumbed it out. *Phew. That was close. But where is the Battle Bugle?*

52

If I were a horn, where would I be?

Zora didn't know a lot about military structure, but she understood enough to know that if the chameleon didn't have it, perhaps another commander did. She crept along the tent, spying the nearest dragons. They were all grands. Men and women slept among them too. She assumed they were the commanders.

Great, there's at least a dozen of them spread out. She spotted the bright eyes of some of the dragons still open. She couldn't even tell whether they were sleeping or not.

Might as well search them all. She started toward the nearest one and stopped. Out of the corner of her eye, she saw Firestok, Justus's dragon, asleep. She backed up and decided to search her first.

Zora almost gasped aloud when she spotted the bugle strung up along the saddle with the dragon's other gear. She approached.

Gooseberries! The bugle hung high up on Firestok's back. It wasn't completely out of reach, but it would be a stretch. *Of all the days I needed to be taller.*

There was a bare spot of ground between the dragon's front paw and Firestok's body. The gap was just big enough for Zora's small feet. She stepped into it one foot at a time and raised on tiptoes.

Here goes. Zora opened up her satchel and took out the leather wrap. She unfolded the package, and without touching a single scale, stuffed the goo into the bell of the bugle. The dragon didn't stir as she packed it in deeper.

Please stay invisible. Please stay invisible. Everything she did was by her sense of touch. It wasn't easy to master, but she'd used the scarf so much that she'd become used to it. Exhaling, she lowered back down on her heels then stepped backward over the dragon's paw.

Firestok's chest rose and fell. She breathed easy.

I did it! Yes!

She placed the leather wrap back inside the satchel and started to walk away, unseen.

Then the tip of Firestok's tail flicked out at Zora's feet. She jumped it, but it was too late.

Firestok looked right at her and said in a hushed voice, "I know you are there, little mouse. State your business, or I'll alert the entire camp."

"As you wish, Firestok," Zora whispered.

Firestok's horns titled as her head rose. "Strange that you speak my name. You've sparked my curiosity. Come closer."

So long as Zora didn't attack, she would remain concealed. She reached into the satchel and grabbed one of the dragon charms. "I'm right here," she said into Firestok's earhole. "You don't know me, but I am Zora, a friend of Cinder's."

"Cinder knows no such name," the lovely eyed dragon said.

"Please, hear me out first. If you don't believe my story, expose me."

Firestok nodded.

Zora said, "Justus is not the one you know. He is a chameleon hiding his identity behind a dragon charm. It places a veil over your eyes. Search deep in your heart—you will know I am right." She shared more intimate knowledge about Zanna Paydark, Olgstern Stronghair, and even Cinder's mother, Bonfire.

Firestok's eyes grew with every piece of information. "I cannot resist my lord's commands."

"You can with this." Zora pulled out her dragon charm. It flickered, and her invisibility faded. "It's a dragon charm. As Tatiana explained to me, one can cancel out the other. "I'll place it under your saddle. It will give you the protection you need."

"I don't know." Firestok eyed the stone.

"What do you have to lose? When the battle begins tomorrow and Justus appears, you will know the truth," Zora said as she crouched down.

"Firestok, who do you speak with?" the false Justus called from the tent.

Firestok nudged Zora, no longer invisible, underneath her wing. "Merely alerting the others that you sensed a presence, Justus."

The chameleon pulled aside the tent flap and looked over the camp. "See to it they are thorough. Something stinks about this night. The last thing we need is one of Black Frost's spies in our camp. Triple the patrol."

"As you wish."

Justus buckled on his sword belt. "We need to spread the word fast. I'll help." He marched away.

Firestok turned her neck around her body. "You aren't going anywhere now, part elf. They'll find you, invisible or not. The dragons are bloodhounds when it comes to sniffing the living out."

"What should I do?"

"I'll cradle you under my wing. Be quiet. Be still."

Zora nodded.

Firestok tucked her away in a nook between her wing and her back.

Zora stuffed the dragon charm deep underneath Firestok's saddle. Her body bounced as Firestok wandered through the camp, gathering patrols and alerting them to a potential intruder.

I hope I am not a complete fool. Firestok could be taking me into the midst of them.

Several minutes passed before the dragon came to a stop. She opened up her wing and stuck her nose in Zora's face.

"There is a pile of dragon dung over there, on the outskirts of camp. Hide in it until we are gone. You might have made your way in, but you won't make your way out. The patrols are ready."

Zora dropped down to the ground and spied the huge pile of dragon manure. Her nose crinkled. "Are you sure there isn't a better way?"

Firestok shook her head. "Not if you want to live."

Dawn broke. The Sky Rider army lifted off and vanished in the sky.

Gorva, Jumax, and Snags wandered through the campground, searching for Zora.

Jumax picked up a feather that had fallen from his wing. "I'm certain she is alive, love."

"Or eaten." There was a deep frown on her face as she hurried across the campground.

A shambling figure wandered their way. Gorva lowered her spear, then Jumax shielded her body with his.

She brushed him aside with her spear. "Out of my way."

The figure approached on stiff legs.

"Zora!"

The part elf was covered head to toe in dry dung. Zora wiped excrement away from her body. "It might look like me, but I'll never be the same again." She raked crust out of her hair. "Mission complete."

Jumax planted his fists on his hips, tossed back his head, and let out a gusty laugh. "Ah ha ha ha!" He threw his arm over Zora's shoulder. "I admire the grit in this one. Stinky but special!"

53

At daybreak, Dark Mountain shone on the distant horizon. The rising sunbeams sparkled on the icy snowcaps.

Grey Cloak rubbed his tingling fingertips on his cloak. His breath was frosty when he spoke. "It might be cold now, but it will be hot really soon."

"Aye, brother. Aye," Dyphestive said.

Talon and their mounts, the children of Cinder, had flown all night long. They'd used their enchanted harnesses to the fullest extent and had hidden in the rocky climbs scattered all over the terrain south of Dark Mountain.

The invading Sky Rider army would arrive soon. The battle would be on.

Justus approached Dyphestive, helmet on and bugle in hand. "I'd prefer to ride on Rock if you'd so oblige. I'll be able to sell my position better on a grand."

"That's fine by me, but I suggest you spend time with Rock first. He's not fond of passengers." Dyphestive smiled and offered his hand. "Best to you, Justus."

Justus nodded. "You as well, Son of Stronghair."

"Remember, we have no way of knowing whether Zora pulled it off or not, and there is no fallback plan," Grey Cloak reminded the older warrior. "But I have faith it will be done."

"I'll convince them all, one way or the other, or die trying." Justus strode away and joined up with Anya and Cinder.

The rest of Talon gathered with the Blood Brothers. Tatiana was the first to speak. "You have a bold plan, Grey Cloak. But I've yet to ask how you came up with the idea."

"Back at Sulter Slay when we battled Commander Azzark's forces, in desperation, Mother and I fused our wizard fire together and shred the dragons in the sky." He wiggled the Rod of Weapons. "Azzark backed off, but what he didn't know was that we were chained."

Yuri wandered into the group. "A chain of fire is brilliant." She showed her charred hands. "But it might burn us all alive. It's risky."

"We'll channel it through the Rod of Weapons. There is no other choice available to us. We can only hope that it will stand up to the heat." Grey Cloak smirked and looked at Dark Mountain. "Black Frost is far from his full strength, not yet the behemoth of the skies that struck down Hidemark. We'll use the combined strength of myself, Yuri, and Anya's wizard fire, along with the power of the rod and Tatiana's Star of Light. We'll draw all of the magic that we can hold while the dragons distract Black Frost with their attacks."

"Good to hear. I hated to think that I was going to stand around and do nothing," Razor said. "Of course, I could always wait for Gorva and her new love to return." He snaked out his swords, spun them both with his wrists, then stuffed them back in their sheaths. "No, I'd rather kill something."

"I'm concerned about Black Frost's magic resistance," Tatiana said with a worried look. "I believe he feeds on Nath's world. And the temple harnesses it. There's a chance our might wouldn't have any effect at all."

Grey Cloak spoke to all. "Well, I'll take my chances. What about the rest of you?"

"Ride the sky, baby!" Streak said. "I'm ready to go."

"Yes, as are we all," Fenora added.

"Then there is only one thing left to do," Grey Cloak said. "Wait."

Dyphestive took his brother aside. With his arm over his shoulder, he said, "Today, we are going to finish this."

"I know I can count on you most of all." Grey Cloak handed Dyphestive a rolled-up bundle.

"What's this?"

"The Cloak of Legends. I have a feeling you are going to need it more than me. After all, you are leading the attack on Black Frost. We will try to punch a hole in him from the deck. You know what to do. Put it on."

Dyphestive nodded. His brow raised when the cloak stretched out over his shoulders. "It fits."

"I'm glad. I wasn't sure he would work with you, but now we know." Grey Cloak rubbed the brick-red sleeves of his shoulders. "Zooks. It's freezing cold."

Dyphestive wiggled inside his new garment. "Not me. I feel snuggly."

"Don't get used to it." He bumped forearms with his brother. "I'll need it back when this is over."

Dyphestive smirked. "We'll see about that."

54

The invading Sky Riders appeared in the south before the break of midday. They moved in a V formation several rows deep, forming a wedge led by the imposter of Justus himself.

From his spot in the cottony veil of clouds above, Justus and Rock waited. To the north, Black Frost's Riskers shot up out of the peaks of Dark Mountain and formed a smaller but identical thunder of dragons.

"That's a lot of dragons." Rock snorted smoke, puffing out of his nostrils. "I think we can take them all."

"I like your spirit. A true son of Cinder, but we don't need to do that. We only need to take one."

Justus studied the ranks. He spotted Hogrim and Hammerjaw, two brothers he'd always been close to. He hoped they were truly on his side. *I'll know soon enough.* In the case of the betrayers, only they knew who was who. When the imposter's bugle sounded, they would separate from the true Sky Riders and trap them between separate armies. "The Battle Bugle has several distinct calls," he explained. "Among the brethren, there is no mistaking their meaning. But it will confuse our enemies, as they will be expecting another call."

Rock's flapping wings kept them hovering. "I don't care for that title, Battle Bugle. I believe 'Death Horn' would be a better fit."

"Hmph. I believe you are right. The Death Horn it is!" Justus removed his helmet and dropped it into the sky. "It's time to get their attention."

"I can't wait to see the looks on their faces." Wings spread, Rock did a nosedive. They glided into the middle of the aerial battlefield, facing the incoming surge of Sky Rider dragons from the south.

Justus saw himself riding in Firestok's saddle and fastened his eyes on his imposter. He waited to see the whites of the chameleon's eyes. When it spotted him, the chameleon's gaze turned blood red.

"I don't think he's very happy to see me," Justus said with a confident grin.

The chameleon raised the bugle to his lips and blew. No sound came. His eyebrows knitted together. He blew again to no avail, lifted it to the sky, then shook it hard.

"Ha! The little thief pulled it off! Beautiful!" Justus locked eyes with Firestok, and he winked three times. It was a silent signal that only the two of them shared, letting the other know they were well. Her pretty eyes lit up, and she grinned with a mouthful of teeth.

Justus returned her smile. "Let chaos reign!"

"I like the sound of that," Rock bellowed. "Blow the Death Horn!"

Justus put the bugle to his lips and blew. The horn's sound shook the clouds. *Paaaaah-poooooh! Pah-pah-paaaah-poooooh!*

All of a sudden, half of the Sky Rider army shot upward in a half loop. To Justus's relief, Hogrim the orc and Hammerjaw the dwarf led the good forces away, separating from the formation of bewildered onlookers. The rest of the wide-eyed army followed the chameleon with confused expressions but remained on course, bearing down on Justus and Rock.

"Ha! The imposters are exposed!" Justus pumped his fist. In addition to Hogrim Hammerjaw, his closest allies, Slomander, Aric, Stayzie, and Mayzie led the true Sky Riders away from the wicked thunder of dragons. Justus's heart leaped. "Today will be a glorious day!"

The chameleon stood up in his stirrups with his finger pointing at Justus, shouting with red-faced rage, "Kill him! Kill him!"

All of a sudden, Firestok flipped upside down. The gallant dragon barrel-rolled like a twisting top, slinging the chameleon clear out of his saddle. She dropped out of the front of the formation, dove after the chameleon, caught the fiend in midair with her jaws, then clamped down.

The chameleon's bones cracked like twigs, and his flesh squished between her teeth.

"That's my dragon!" Seeing the confusion in the false Sky Rider's faces, Justus called to Rock, "Join the others!"

Rock twisted his head around and said, "But I want to fight!"

"Don't worry, they'll come! Ride the sky, Rock! Ride the sky!"

STANDING up in the stirrups of his grand dragon's saddle, Hogrim looked over at Hammerjaw and shouted, "Something is amiss! I thought this day had stink all over it, and now we know those are defectors!"

"Can you be certain?" the potbellied dwarf Hammerjaw shouted back. He lifted his tremendous battle-ax with its bright glowing blade.

Hogrim wiped his nose across his forearm and eyed the dragon riders joining the ranks of the Riskers. The burly orc stuffed himself into a suit of full-metal armor and spat over the side of the dragon's saddle. "Can there be any doubt?"

The elven siblings Arik, Stayzie, and Mayzie, along with the lizardman Slomander, joined them in the sky.

"Are we betrayed?" Arik asked, with his perfectly polished armor shining in the sun.

Hogrim nodded.

"What do we do?" Stayzie asked with her eyebrows knitted together.

"Listen to the Battle Bugle's call!" Hogrim said. "That's our fight song! I believe Justus plays it. He was always terrible on the horn."

Pah-Pooh! Pah-Pooh-Pah-Pooh! Pah-Pooh! Pah-Pooh-Pah-Pooh! The bugle sounded again.

Hammerjaw raised his ax higher. "Ride the Sky!"

Dragons roared. The last regiment of the Sky Rider army gathered behind them, forming a wedge behind their leaders. All together, the army shouted, "Ride the Sky! Death to Black Frost and his legions!"

The Sky Riders, outnumbered two to one, flew toward the enemy on thundering wings and rained down chaos beneath the clouds of mystical wildfire and dragon flame.

GREY CLOAK WATCHED the scene in the sky from afar. It was a thing of beauty. The Sky Riders split apart from the pack at the sound of Justus's horn.

"She did it," he said with a clenched fist. "Zora pulled it off. Perfect!"

The faithful dragon riders slipped out of the trap and regrouped in the south. Meanwhile, the evil forces of Black Frost merged with the traitors and gave chase.

Grey Cloak's company had moved to the base of Black Frost's temple, undetected during the confusion. They'd split into four small groups, one on each side of the ziggurat, where the dragons dug their claws into the stone and climbed the icy walls like sand lizards.

Grey Cloak rode on Streak, Tatiana in the saddle behind him.

"I don't know about you," she said, "but my skin prickles all over."

"I know the feeling. One would think we'd be used to it by now."

Streak turned his head around and flicked his pink tongue. "I want to get this over with. Then it will be popcorn and milkshakes for everyone!"

"What is he talking about?" Tatiana asked.

"He likes to babble about his journey to another world."

"Oh."

"No, I'm breaking the tension," Streak said with a quick rustle of his wings. "The two of you are stiff as boards. Loosen up so we can defeat Black Frost. I'm sick of hearing his name."

"Agreed," Grey Cloak and Tatiana said together. They didn't always get along, but over the course of the quest, they'd come to trust and respect one another. "It's been an honor adventuring with you," both of them said at the same time. They laughed.

"Who'd have ever thought we'd become so familiar?" she said.

"Agreed. Miracles do happen."

Streak crested the top of the temple and climbed over the last wall.

Black Frost sat in the dead center of the temple, surveying the ascending heroes. The blazing blue-eyed, black-scaled dragon was no longer the gargantuan size they were used to, but his body was still at least four times the size of the largest grand.

Fenora and Bellarose with Rhonna and the dwarves emerged on the northern side behind Black Frost. Smash and Chubby climbed up on the eastern end, and Razor and Slicer appeared on the west side along with Feather and Shannon.

Behind Streak, Cinder and Anya came with Nath and Yuri riding with them.

"Welcome, strangers," Black Frost said in a voice full of thunder. "Your death awaits."

55

Grey Cloak jumped down from Streak's saddle. "No! Today, your Day of Betrayal ends." The tip of the Rod of Weapons blossomed into a blue spear point. Tatiana, Yuri, and Anya joined his side. "No need to surrender, Black Frost. We aren't taking any prisoners."

"The flea has a sharp tongue." Black Frost's eyes swept over all of the dragons on the temple top. "I'm not familiar with the other insects aside from you, Cinder. Did you come to witness their glorious deaths as well as your own?"

Cinder replied, "Your voice trembles, wicked one. You're confused, aren't you?"

"Tremble. Ha." Black Frost raised a paw and flexed his claws. "There is nothing to fear. I tremble with power—omnipotent power, world-rending power, beyond anything you can comprehend."

"You've got that wrong," Anya said with a snarl on her face.

Black Frost snorted. "I don't know where you come from, but it won't make any difference. I am invincible." His chest scales heated up. "And nothing can withstand my breath"—he glanced up, where a squad of dragons descended on their position with teeth and claws bared—"or my elite guardians." He flashed his great teeth. "Nothing can surprise me. I'm prepared for everything."

Grey Cloak gave Cinder the nod.

"Children, attack!"

Half of Cinder's children took to the sky, led by Razor and Shannon. The others charged Black Frost with fire and flame.

"This is it. Now!" Grey Cloak braced his feet and pointed the Rod of Weapons at Black Frost. Yuri and Tatiana linked up on one of his arms, and Anya took the other.

Anchoring the end of the chain, Tatiana held the pink Star of Light and fed her energy into Yuri, who passed it next into Grey Cloak. On his right, Anya fed her wizard fire into him. He absorbed all of their power, holding it as long as he could. A bright light blossomed all around them. Their skin glowed like fire. The Rod of Weapons turned white in his hands.

"Let it loose, Grey!" Anya shouted. "Or you'll cook yourself alive!"

"We're only getting one shot at this," he said, his voice cracking. "I'm not taking any chances. We're hitting him with all we have! Everything we've got now!"

Dragons jumped on Black Frost's body, biting, clawing, and

releasing their flames. He whipped them aside with a flick of his tail and swatted them away like pups.

With eyes of fire, Grey Cloak unleashed the awesome funnel of power. A huge bolt of energy streaked across the temple's roof and slammed into Black Frost's massive bulk.

The huge dragon skidded backward with his claws ripping up the stones. He let out a painful roar, braced himself, and pushed back.

Grey Cloak lost the channel of energy, and the tip of the Rod of Weapons cooled.

"My magic is far too strong! Feel my wrath!" Black Frost let loose his dragon breath.

"Shield, Tatiana! Everyone, channel your energy to her!"

The Star of Light created a pink dome that covered all of them. Black Frost washed the mystic barrier in azure flames.

Sweat dripped into Grey Cloak's eyes. His wizard fire was being sapped. "Keep it up, everyone! A little longer!"

Black Frost towered over the dome. His scorching dragon breath started eating through the shield. Holes opened. Fire bled through.

The hair on Grey Cloak's arms started to curl.

Yuri groaned.

"We can't hold this forever!" Anya said.

Grey Cloak searched the skies but could barely see through the flickering flames. "Oh, brother, where are you?"

A voice from above carried over the roar of the flames, drawing Black Frost's attention away. "It's thunder time!"

Dyphestive was falling out of the sky with the great Iron

Sword gripped in his hands. The blood-red gemstone shone like a hot sun. The Sword of Chaos came alive in his hands.

Black Frost turned his fire on the falling warrior, who had a berserker's look in his eyes. Blue fire swallowed Dyphestive whole.

The Blood Brother's plunge into the fiery depths didn't slow. Flesh burned from his fingers as he streaked down through the flames. He brought the sword down in a flash. The white-hot blade cut deep into Black Frost's neck, penetrating iron-hard scales, muscle, and bone.

The blue flames died as Dyphestive smashed into the roof.

The dragon's head dangled from the partially severed neck, but the cut hadn't gone clean through. Black Frost, dangling head and all, still breathed.

"No! We must finish him! Feed me your power!" Grey Cloak commanded.

The chain of heroes reversed their energy from the shield and pushed it back into Grey Cloak. He absorbed the surge of renewed wizard fire, summoned from the depths of their inner strength.

Black Frost's neck started to mend. Scale and flesh pulled together as one.

Grey Cloak let loose all of his firepower. *Shhhraaat!*

The deadly funnel of energy sliced through Black Frost's neck, severing it cleanly. His head dropped onto the temple floor. It rolled to a stop, right side up.

They hit Black Frost's face with all of their combined might. Their fire burned out the dragon's eyes, burrowed into his skull, and shot out of his earholes. He kept going until there was nothing left but remnants of scales and a tremendous smoking head. The rod's light sputtered out.

He gasped and fell down on his knees. The others collapsed beside him.

Still burning, Black Frost spoke, "You cannot kill me. Nothing can kill me. I am invincible!"

Grey Cloak spotted his brother. Dyphestive, covered in blisters, climbed to his feet and picked up his sword. "Go, brother," he panted as sweat dripped into his eyes. "Do it."

"Indestructible! Indomitable!" Black Frost's voice grew in strength. "Hahahaha! This is only the beginning!"

Dyphestive gripped the Iron Sword by the handle with fingers showing more bone than skin. Staggering, he dragged the great blade, scraping across the roof's stones. With his skin smoldering, smoke rising from burnt hair and shoulders, and his face burnt to a crisp and blistered, he climbed up between the horns on Black Frost's head.

"What are you doing? Get off of me!" Black Frost moaned as flaming blue eyes formed inside sockets and looked up.

Raising the blade with two hands, Dyphestive turned it down, and said, "Say your last words, dragon!"

"I am unstop—*urk*!"

Dyphestive drove the blade home, deep into the dragon's skull. Fire shot out of every orifice. A concussive pulse ripped across the rooftop like a great wind. The flames in Black Frost's eyes went dark.

"Did we do it?" Dyphestive looked at his brother and asked.

Grey Cloak gave him an uncertain shrug and said, "I suppose. I told you I'd think of something."

Dyphestive managed an ugly smile through his scorched face as his skin started to heal as he hopped down to the ground. He looked back at the smoking skull and said, "Should I get my sword?"

"No!" Grey Cloak, Tatiana, Anya, and Yuri answered. "Not yet," Grey Cloak added.

With exhausted looks, they watched the monumental skull of Black Frost burn. Scales fell away from flesh and muscle until nothing was left but bone and the smoke rising from it. Black Frost's body burned up as well, leaving only bones as his remains.

Wiping the sweat from his brow, Grey Cloak rose to one knee, spun the rod, and stood before Black Frost's smoking face. He said with a smirk, "Well, you weren't prepared for that, were you, Black Frost?" He looked at his brother and said, "I think it's safe to say that it's over."

Dyphestive crossed his arms and nodded. "Agreed."

Grey Cloak joined his drained comrades, Tatiana, Yuri, and Anya. "That was incredible. Are all of you well?"

"Numb but breathing," Anya answered. Cinder gathered himself by her side and licked her face. She patted his snout. "Give me a moment while I catch my breath so we can go after those traitors."

"No, we'll have to leave that to Justus and the rest of the Sky Riders. We need to find a way back to our own time," Tatiana said. "It won't be easy, but at least we have knowledge that we didn't have before. We'll either have to rebuild the Time Mural or wait out our lives in Safe Haven."

"For the next twenty years." Grey Cloak shook his head. "I don't think so."

BY THE TIME the smoke cleared, everyone from Zora to Jumax, Cinder, and his children gathered on the top of the temple. The Riskers fled after a brief battle, according to Justus. "Their spines broke the instant they learned Black Frost had fallen. Now it's our mission to put an end to the rest of them."

Zora rejoined her friends with a warm embrace and a huge smile on her face. As every man and dragon reunited in victory, another stranger appeared who had escaped their attention. Zora nudged Grey Cloak, her mouth half agape. "Uh, who is that?"

A man stood among the group, unlike any they'd seen before. The women stared at him with big eyes. Even Gorva and Anya couldn't seem to tear their eyes away. He stood as tall as Dyphestive, broad-shouldered and striking. His eyes shone like gold coins and long, blood-red hair hung down over his shoulders onto his broad chest. A chiseled frame showed cords of muscle underneath a tattered set of robes. His arms were covered from fingertip to neck in obsidian-colored scales. He was a vision of health and beauty and spoke in a voice as pure as melted silver.

"I am grateful to all of you, each and every one. Your courage not only saved the day, but it saved me and my homeworld," the newcomer said.

"Nath?" Grey Cloak asked with an astonished expression.

Zora added with a startled look, "Whoa."

Streak moseyed over to Nath, sniffed him, then licked his face. "Yup, it's the crusty old hermit. I'd recognize him anywhere. I'm glad to see you looking fit, more like the first time we met."

Grey Cloak and Dyphestive shared a confused look. They walked over to Nath and shook his hand. "You can return home now?"

"Aye." Nath clamped his hands on the outside of their shoulders. "Thanks to you. Thanks to all of you!" He chuckled. "I never doubted you for a minute."

All of the women, starting with Gorva and ending with Yuri, lined up and gave him a warm, loving embrace.

The men congregated, watching in fascination, and Jumax said, "What is this all about?"

Razor laughed. "Ha. How's that treat you?"

Nath waved goodbye once more, petting all of the dragons as he went, then descended into the temple where the gateway to his world waited. "Blood Brothers, don't fret. I'll free your parents before I go."

Grey Cloak and Dyphestive gave Tatiana a desperate look.

"Your parents will be fine," she said, "but we must leave. The longer we stay, the more danger to our time. And there will be changes. Extraordinary ones, I imagine."

Reluctantly, Grey Cloak and Dyphestive climbed onto their

dragons, but they took their time about it. As they made their way to the wall, they took one last look back.

Zanna and Jerrik Paydark emerged from the temple stairwell. Olgstern Stronghair appeared behind them, with shoulders so broad his shadow swallowed the other two up.

Grey Cloak and Dyphestive waved and offered childish smiles as they captured their parents' confused yet thankful expressions. After their comrades, off to Safe Haven they went, knowing in their heart of hearts that they hadn't saved just a few —they'd saved them all.

56

CONCLUSION

A FEW SEASONS AFTER TATIANA—WITH THE HELP OF THE WIZARD Watch—had returned the heroes to their time, many of them reunited on Raven Cliff in the Red Claw Tavern. At a large oak table in the back, Dyphestive sat elbow to elbow with the pitted-faced Browning on one side and the former Monarch Knight and Shannon's father, Adanadel, on the other.

Shannon walked over from the bar with her hands full, three tankards of ale in each. She took the open seat beside her father and shoved the beers down the table. "Drink up, men! And I'm not buying the next round." She looked at Razor, who danced his way over with more drinks. "My husband is."

Dyphestive guzzled his down in one swallow. His face was fuller since his blond beard had grown in, though he kept it trimmed, and he'd matured many years. He hammered the table with his fist. "I'll take another!"

"You'll need another and another, considering who you are marrying tomorrow," Grey Cloak said. He'd been sitting quietly at the table's end, watching his friends celebrate. He smirked at his brother. "Your days are going to get a lot, well, fuller, if you know what I mean."

Zora elbowed him. "What is that supposed to mean?"

"Nothing, love. I mean, marriage is the best thing that ever happened to me, but, you know, he's marrying—"

"Ha! Look who is here!" Dyphestive rose so fast he bumped the table with his knees, spilling ale everywhere. "Jakoby! Tinison! Leena! I didn't think you'd make it!"

He climbed over the table and embraced all except the black-robed Leena. The bright-redheaded monk from the Ministry of Hoods cocked back her fist when he tried. He extended his hand. "It's always good to see you, Leena."

She nodded, walked away, then sat down behind a table, her face blank.

Zora whispered in Grey Cloak's ear, "I think someone still has a soft spot for her."

"The big ox has a soft spot for everybody." He kissed his wife on the cheek. "You know, I'm a little jealous of him."

"Why is that?"

"Because," he said with a smile, "I wouldn't mind getting married to you again."

Zora's face softened. She pinched his chin. "You have gotten to be quite the charmer. Keep improving. I like it."

With her hand in his, Grey Cloak watched the reunion of friends unfold. Many were once dead, but now alive again, healthy and with smiles on their faces and full of color. Crane escorted friend after friend inside, including Leena, Jakoby, and Sergeant Tinison. Zora's mentor, Tanlin, was back. The inseparable Jumax and Gorva were present, hand in hand as she sat on his lap at a nearby table. Grunt the minotaur crammed his way inside, and the last arrivals were Tatiana and Dalsay, once again living in the flesh.

"I need to pinch myself," Grey Cloak said. "I have goosebumps all over."

Zora hugged his arm. "So do I. Everyone seems so happy, so peaceful."

Grey Cloak nodded. "If it could only stay this way."

"Well, someone has to protect the world so that others can have days like this," she said. "It might as well be us. I believe that is what we are here for."

Dyphestive pounded another round of ale in a race with Browning. He beat him soundly.

"Gar!" Browning spoke in slobbering words. "The only man that can outdrink me."

Dyphestive plopped down in a chair beside his brother. "Are yew st-st-still g-g-going to be me bestss man?"

"Are you slurring?" Grey Cloak laughed. "Brother, you are a horrible actor. Can you even get drunk?"

Dyphestive shrugged. "I suppose not. But I enjoy trying."

"Tomorrow's the big day. Are you sure that you want to go through with it?"

"Of course I am. I'm looking forward to it, aren't you?"

"I'm looking forward to beating the bushes and bringing

down old enemies. Our friends might live, but our enemies live again as well."

Zora elbowed Grey Cloak. "Let it go. It's time to celebrate. Dyphestive, I am very excited for you and your big day tomorrow."

"Thank you, Zora. I wish my brother was as excited as you."

Grey Cloak smirked. "It's a wedding. Don't expect me to be all mushy about it."

"That's not how you sounded earlier," Zora said.

"What can I say? I can be exceptionally charming when I want to be."

"I'll remember that. If you'll excuse me, I'm going to talk with Tatiana." Zora gave Dyphestive a peck on the cheek then left.

"Truly, brother, you couldn't find a more compatible woman. She understands you and our cause. It will be a special union," Grey Cloak said. "So, who is going to carry who across the threshold?"

"Ha," Dyphestive grunted.

Browning, Adanadel, Shannon, Jakoby, Razor, and Tinison all burst out laughing.

"A good one, Grey Cloak!" the fuzzy-headed Tinison said in his loud voice. "So, who carries who, Dyphestive?"

"It doesn't matter to me. I like a strong woman. It will be interesting to see whether she can lift me." Dyphestive smiled then lifted his tankard. "To Talon!"

Everyone else lifted a pint and chanted, "Talon! Talon! Talon!"

Grey Cloak overheard two curmudgeons sitting nearby say,

"See what happens when you let in too many swords and sorcerers?"

He had to laugh at that.

"What are you chuckling about?" Dyphestive asked.

"Nothing. Just promise me you won't make the honeymoon too long. And don't spawn a bushel of little farmers either. I need you. There will always be a remnant causing trouble if we don't do anything about it. The Riskers run wild. Deviant dragons and naturals are loose."

"I know." Dyphestive nudged his brother with his elbow. "If there's one thing we learned from Nath, it is this—there is only one way to defeat evil. Hunt it down and stomp it to death."

Grey Cloak smirked. "Amen."

Razor stood up and raised his drink. He gave Jumax and Gorva a quick approving nod then eyed Dyphestive. "And you'll have the perfect mate for that, brother! To Dyphestive and Anya! Festive and Fiery Red! May they run roughshod over the wicked all the livelong day! Wah-hoo!"

Everyone lifted up their mugs then clacked them together, sloshing foamy ale down the sides and dripping onto the floor.

Dyphestive was all smiles. The sight of his brother so happy warmed Grey Cloak's heart too. He stood up and said, "Say, let's take a walk outside and see what the others are doing. I could use the fresh air. It's starting to stink here, and I'm not certain whether it's Grunt or you."

"It's Grunt. Even I don't smell that bad on my worst day."

They pushed through the chairs and tables to the front door

and made their way out of the Red Claw Tavern. A blast of wind cooled their faces.

"Ah, that's better!" Grey Cloak walked across the deck of iron planks and made it to the railing. The wide metal walkway was mounted to the side of a sheer cliff that overlooked the open plains, catching the last rays of daylight below. "I love this view."

Dyphestive joined his side. "Agreed." He looked beyond his oversized hands on the rails at the dragons, frolicking like puppies in the fields. "Look at them. Who would have ever thought we'd be Sky Riders one day?"

Firestok and Cinder were there with all of their children. The grands, Rock, Snags, Bellarose, Smash, Chubbs, and Fenora, couldn't be missed as they splashed away in the lake, with hundreds of farmers watching. The smaller middlings were there too. Feather, Slicer, and Slick, the triplets, raced through the sky, even giving rides to children.

All but one of the dragons could be seen having a festival of their own. As Grey Cloak searched, he saw no sign of Streak.

"Hmm... it seems one of the groomsmen is missing," Grey Cloak said.

Dyphestive leaned over the railing. "That's strange. He was with them when I came in." He shrugged. "Don't worry about it. He'll show up soon. He's not one to miss out on a party. Goy, look!" He spun Grey Cloak by the shoulders.

"Easy." He spied a group of people coming down the stairs that led up to the streets of Raven Cliff. His throat tightened. "I'll be. I didn't expect them, you know, with their important missions with the Wizard Watch."

"I guess they aren't old enough to call it quits." Dyphestive rubbed his brother's shoulders and studied the mountain of a man that was Olgstern Stronghair, his father, coming down the steps with his lovely mother hooked on one massive arm. "Who do you think is bigger, me or my father?"

"Your father is much bigger."

"Is not. You only say that to get my goat."

"Works every time." Grey Cloak spied his own parents, Zanna and Jerrik Paydark, walking behind the Stronghairs. He'd never seen his mother smile so much while laughing at his father's words. There was no question. They were happy. "Tomorrow will truly be a special day." His eyes watered. "We're all together, and no more funerals for a change."

"Hear, hear," Dyphestive said.

Something large landed behind them. They turned and found themselves face-to-face with a man-sized Streak.

"There you are," Grey Cloak said. "I was beginning to worry. Whoa, how did you become so small? You were full-size only hours ago."

Streak had an impish grin on his face, and his twin tails wagged slowly behind him. Standing like a man, he leaned back with one elbow on the rail. "With Tatiana's help, I've been able to harness my growing power. And I really wanted to make sure I fit in Tanlin's custom-made tuxedo." He tapped his horns. "With a top hat too."

"You don't have growing power," stated Grey Cloak. "She gave you a potion, didn't she?"

"What's a tuxedo?" Dyphestive asked.

Streak addressed them both one at a time. "I *do* have growing power. And you'll see what a tuxedo is tomorrow." His glance moved toward the stairs and brightened. "Oh, here comes Anya. You can't see her before the wedding." He started pushing Dyphestive back inside. "In you go, big boy."

"But I want to see her."

Grey Cloak escorted his brother toward the door. "I'll let her know that you miss her. Now, back inside you go."

"Fine, I'm going," he said, stealing a glimpse of his soon-to-be wife. "I told you I would marry her, didn't I?" He nudged Grey Cloak with his big elbow.

"Yes, only about a hundred times over the last few days."

"Tell her I love her."

Grey Cloak smirked. "Yeah, that's definitely not going to come from me."

Streak and Dyphestive vanished inside, and the bowels of the tavern exploded in raucous cheers for Streak.

"I have to admit, he knows how to work a room." Grey Cloak's eyes met Anya's. Her striking sun-bleached hair cascaded over well-tanned shoulders. Her white sundress, made by Tanlin, softened her rugged exterior and enhanced her natural beauty. He managed a smile and waved.

Anya waved back and joined the procession of parents. They all embraced in warm hugs and greetings.

Zora slipped outside and wrapped her arm around his waist, cozying up to him. "How are you? Your eyes look a little misty?"

"It's from the smoke you brought from inside."

"Sure it is." She squeezed him. "Speaking of Smoke, it's a

shame some of our friends from the other worlds couldn't make it."

Grey Cloak reached inside the Cloak of Legends and pulled out the Figurine of Heroes. He smirked. His dark eyes twinkled. "Perhaps some of them can make it?"

"Oh, no you don't! You tried that trick at our wedding." She tried to grab it, but he was too quick. "Remember how that turned out? We almost missed our honeymoon."

"Yes." He grinned as he eyed the figurine. "It was a day I'll never forget."

First and foremost, thank you for reading all the way to the very end! It means a lot! Now, if you will, slap down a REVIEW of Dark Mountain: Dragon Wars Book #20. LINK!

Friends,

There are so many things I want to say about the completion of this series. Man, I've never tackled a 2 year, 20-book, 1 million word project before, but I am happy to say to me, myself and I ... WE DID IT!

. . .

AND IF I didn't have readers like you sticking with me throughout the process, it might never have been done. I do it for all of you, whether it's a handful, or bushels of readers, I'm honored that you enjoy my stories.

So MUCH TOO UNFOLD THOUGH, and many of you might not be sure where to go next, if you are new to my works, that is. I definitely took liberty of finding a creative way to introduce you to my worlds in other works. I think it was so much fun, using Time Mural Chamber to allow time/portal travel between different worlds of which I have many.

THE FIGURINE OF HEROES was a blast to use, and bring in some familiar faces for longstanding devout readers, and add an element of excitement for new readers. It made the entire series more exciting for me to write as well, as I miss writing about many of our fantasy friends, even the villainous ones. A shame that there is never enough time for all of them. That being said, using these new and surprising elements allowed me to push my imagination further, and I certainly foresee more inter-world activity with these heroes in the future.

TO CLARIFY, all of my worlds are connected together in one way or another, so there will be many tie-ins where I can see the Figurine of Heroes, Wizard Watch, and even the Time Mural

Chamber having an impact in other worlds, and quite possibly they might be making an appearance in the continuation of The Supernatural Bounty Hunter Files and The Henchmen Chronicles, which are being web strung together as we speak.

IN THE MEANTIME, see my complete book list below for links to my other numerous works, at least 80 more books of reading available, over 3 million more words. All of them tie-in to Dragon Wars in one way or the other. And if you have any questions, please, drop me a line anytime at: craig@thedarkslayer.com.

RIDE THE SKY,

CRAIG

OH, I do plan on putting this series on audio as well. Thanks!

AND IF YOU haven't already, signup for my newsletter and grab 3 FREE books including the Dragon Wars Prequel.
WWW.DRAGONWARSBOOKS.COM

TEACHERS AND STUDENTS, if you would like to order paperback copies for you library or classroom, email craig@thedarkslayer.com to receive a special discount.

GEAR UP in this Dragon Wars body armor enchanted with a +2 Coolness factor/+4 at Gaming Conventions. Sizes range from halfling (Small) to Ogre (XXL). LINK . www.society6.com

CRAIG'S COMPLETE BOOK LIST

OVER 100 TITLES! PURE ADRENALINE!

5 MILLION WORDS IN PUBLICATION!

EPIC FANTASY, SWORD AND SORCERY URBAN FANTASY, SCI-FI, POST-APOC! LINKS BELOW!

FREE BOOKS

The Darkslayer: Brutal Beginnings

Nath Dragon – Quest for the Thunderstone

The Henchmen Chronicles Intro

Dragon Wars Prequel

The Odyssey of Nath Dragon Series (Prequel to Chronicles of Dragon)

Exiled: Book 1 of 5

The Odyssey of Nath Dragon Boxset (Best Deal)

The Chronicles of Dragon Series 1 (10 Books)

The Hero, the Sword and the Dragons (Book 1)

Boxset 1-5

Boxset 6-10

Collector's Edition 1-10 (Best Deal)

Tail of the Dragon, The Chronicles of Dragon, Series 2 (10 book series)

Tail of the Dragon Book #1

Boxset 1-5

Boxset 6-10

Collector's Edition 1-10 (Best Deal)

The Darkslayer Series 1 – 6 books

Wrath of the Royals (Book 1)

Boxset 1-3

Boxset 4-6

Omnibus 1-6 (Best Deal)

The Darkslayer: Bish and Bone, Series 2 (10 Book series)

Bish and Bone (Book 1 of 10)

Boxset 1-5

Boxset 6-10

Bish and Bone Omnibus (Books 1-10) (Best Deal)

Dragon Wars: 20-Book Series

Blood Brothers: Book 1 of 20

Boxset 1-5

Boxset 6-10

Boxset 11-15

Boxset 16-20

CLASH OF HEROES: Nath Dragon meets The Darkslayer

Book 1 of 3

Special Edition - Books 1-3 (Best Deal)

The Supernatural Bounty Hunter Files (10 book series)

Smoke Rising: Book 1 of 10

Boxset 1-5

Boxset 6-10

Collector's Edition 1-10 (Best Deal)

The Henchmen Chronicles 5-Book Series

The King's Henchmen - Book 1 of 5

The Henchmen Chronicles Collection: Books 1-5

Zombie Impact Series

Zombie Day Care: Book 1

Zombie Rehab: Book 2

Zombie Warfare: Book 3

Boxset: Books 1-3 (Best Deal)

The Gamma Earth Cycle

Escape from the Dominion

Flight from the Dominion

Prison of the Dominion

The Sorcerer's Power Series

The Sorcerer's Curse: Book 1 of 5

The Red Citadel and the Sorcerer's Power (All 5 Books)

The Misadventures of Dan - Drama/Comedy

Gorgon Thunder-Bot Incinerator of Worlds (1 book, childrens)

ABOUT THE AUTHOR

Check me out on Bookbub and follow: Craig Halloran

I'd love it if you would subscribe to my newsletter and download my free books: www.craighalloran.com/email

On Facebook, you can find me at The Darkslayer Report by Craig Halloran.

Twitter, Twitter, Twitter. I am there, too: www.twitter.com/Craig-Halloran

And of course, you can always email me anytime at craig@thedarkslayer.com

Lightning Source UK Ltd.
Milton Keynes UK
UKHW021838011121
393226UK00003B/355